The Advancement
of
Ignorance

Other Books by William F. Van Wert

Novels

Stool Wives
Don Quickshot
What's It All About?: A Novel About Life, Love, and Key Lime Pie

Short Stories

Tales for Expectant Fathers
Missing in Action

Poems

Vital Signs (forthcoming)
The Invention of Ice Skating
Proper Myth

Essays

Memory Links

Film Criticism

The Theory and Practice of the Ciné-Roman
The Film Career of Alain Robbe-Grillet

The Advancement
of
Ignorance

Stories by

William F. Van Wert

BkMk Press
University of Missouri - Kansas City

MISSOURI ARTS COUNCIL

Financial assistance for this book has been provided by the Missouri Arts Council, a state agency.

Cover design by Bense Garza, Garza Art & Design, Kansas City, Missouri, http://www.garza-artdesign.com
Book design by Roxanne Witt

The author wishes to acknowledge the editors of *California Quarterly, CutBank, Oxford Magazine, Poet and Critic,* and Word Beat Press, which previously published some of the stories that now appear in this collection.

Library of Congress Cataloging-in-Publication Data

Van Wert, William F.
        The advancement of ignorance: stories / by William F. Van Wert.

        p.   cm.
        ISBN 1-886157-19-7
        I.   Title.
        PS3572.A4228A66   1999
        811'.54—dc21   99-19237

                CIP

Printed in Canada   10   9   8   7   6   5   4   3   2   1

for David

Contents

The Advancement of Ignorance

*An Aztec athlete who won a
championship was awarded the
spectator's clothes.*

We'd been robbing Aztec banks from the beginning. Cortez may go down in history books as a passable navigator and a shucks-lucky explorer and discoverer, but me and the boys in the band knew better from the first. Cortez wasn't interested in history. He was interested in loot, and the Aztec bankers wrote the book on loot. Rubies, emeralds, diamonds bigger than thumbnails, even tanzanite. We didn't even bother with the pearl divers down in Acapulco or the live burials in the Yucatán. Balboa could fill his pockets on them. We hit the banks.

The Aztec bankers were a fierce bunch. Primo warriors, most of them, in their younger days. They were proud and sullen. They bowed to each other when they exchanged the keys to one another's till. And they were real snappy dressers. They were the first people to wear white shirts in Mexico. No serape, no sombrero, no siesta. Aztec bankers never lounged. They stood erect at all times. Very tall, very thin, the height of masculinity. In all my days of robbing banks under Cortez, I never caught a single Aztec banker wearing an ascot.

Cortez liked to call them *basura* and *moscas* and *mocos*, pejorative things. I think Cortez had a secret envy of those Aztec bankers, lacking social status himself. There were certain claims of illegitimacy in his family tree, and, I guess, once he got over to the New World, he took it out on the natives. He was forever fond of calling them "bastard Aztec bankers," as though their birthright had anything to do with anything.

Once, we were in this Aztec bank in Sonora and Cortez walked up to this proper-looking teller, not a hint of beard-growth on that tapered, olive face, and Cortez put a hand-cannon on him and says, "Gimme some doubloons." Of course, the Aztec bankers didn't keep doubloons in-house. They traded for them. They had a posted exchange rate for them. But they didn't keep them in the drawers. It was clear to me and the boys in the band that Cortez was trying to pick a fight, with racial overtones.

"You gimme some doubloons," Cortez says, "or I'm gonna turn you into a telescope."

Aztec bankers are very literal. This one didn't seem threatened, because he didn't understand hyperbole.

Cortez cocked both barrels and blew the Aztec banker's head off.

"*La puta madre que te parió*," he says, as though the Aztec banker can still hear him in the spirit world.

When we questioned El Conquistador about the incident, he did not deny his racial prejudices nor his need for random violence.

"They're like the Moors, these Aztec bankers," he said. "They're very prolific. That young teller, for instance. I could tell he was very virile. There's no telling how many Aztecs he would have sired, if I had let him live."

When explanations of the moment didn't satisfy us, then Cortez would resort to the visionary approach, his prophet's leap-frog over history.

"We will not live to see the day, *compañeros*, but mark my words. One day all peoples in Mexico will speak Spanish, because of what we do today. And they will speak good Spanish. They will use subjunctives. Thank you very much. *No sean desgraciados*. Thank you very much."

"*Pelotas*," we all shouted. "*Pelotas*."

His charisma was incredible.

What we didn't know at the time was that Cortez and

Pizarro had made a bet, to see who could conquer first. Pizarro was down South, decimating the Incas with relative ease in Peru. But, of course, that's not what he wrote to Cortez. In his letters to Hernando, Pizarro complained that Peru encompassed half the continent of South America, information that Cortez could not refute. Cortez had already calculated that Mexico encompassed half the North American continent, and yet, to his discredit, he wrote lies to Pizarro, saying that Mexico was larger than the Atlantic Ocean and that Marco Polo would have been lucky to make mailman here.

Neither one knew what the other was really going through, and so scouts were sent from both sides to spy on the other, but none of those scouts ever accomplished a complete round-trip.

The key figure here, of course, was Balboa. He had crossed at Panama and probably had information about both continents. So, both Cortez and Pizarro were constantly inviting Balboa to visit. He never came, though. Apparently, Balboa was a bit eccentric to begin with, and then he felt cheated at the Panama crossing, that there was so little land and so much ocean. He knew monuments would never be named after him, and so he went home disillusioned.

In his sketches of Balboa, Cortez invariably drew him in blackface and gave him the body of a baobab tree.

Once in awhile, Cortez would experience *le cafard mondial*, extreme homesickness, not uncommon among explorers of the day. But, rather than succumb to that melancholy, Cortez would hang Aztec bankers in the public square. Both Spaniards and Aztecs knew the protocol in this instance. If the Aztecs were hung in the usual way, it was because they had been found guilty of crimes. But, if they were hung upside-down, it was because Hernando was homesick. Some of the Aztecs, those who had traveled and, therefore, knew what homesickness was, sent him postcards of bullfights and heaping plates of *paella a la Valenciana*. He was not cheered by these gestures.

In the early days of the Conquest, Aztec banks were as open as a drunkard's throat. And the bankers were interchangeable with the citizens. If a teller were slightly thirsty, for example, a customer might spell him, taking over the till, while the teller went off to enjoy a pot of chamomile tea, a slice of rhubarb pie, a leisurely bit of peyote.

In those same early days, the Aztec bankers assumed that we Spaniards were interchangeable with Aztecs. The tellers would get up and go out for their pot of tea, we would ransack the rubies and emeralds, and there were no casualties on either side. Those were peaceful times.

It came, I think, as a genuine surprise to the Aztec bankers that they had actually been robbed. The concept was unheard of before we came. Indeed, they had no word in their language for *robbery*. Their first fumbling attempts to coin a word for robbery resulted in hyphenations, compound words that roughly translated to the following: surprise-withdrawal, knowing-unknowing, and magic-bankruptcy.

Nor did they have a synonym in their language for lust, or, at least, lust as we practiced it. Aztec women neither ran to us nor away from us. They could go immobile at the snap of a finger. It was true that we raped them in large numbers, but we could never verify it by them. The Aztec women went so deep into their spirit world that they never knew what hit them: not before, nor during, nor after. In fact, the concept of sexuality was unknown to them. They assumed that sexuality, what we called sexuality, was interchangeable with every other aspect of life. A pot of chamomile tea was as "erotic" to them as a woman's breasts falling out as she drew water from the well.

To try to understand these cultural differences, I attended the Aztec cinema. An Aztec banker told me about a particular movie, whose name is too long to translate, which he described as "very hot." I went to see this movie. It consisted of an Aztec man and woman sitting in the desert, watching birds fly by from time to time. For three hours, the Aztec couple sat there, and there were maybe six birds in the whole picture.

Seeing that movie soured my desire for Aztec women, and, for a time, I feared that I had become like the Aztecs. I found myself staring into the glare of the Mexican sun, on the off-chance I might spot a robin or raven or redbird. I began seeing auras, and that's when Cortez threatened to shoot me. He saved my life, even though he never understood my malady. He assumed that I was suffering from homesickness.

The Aztecs were similarly resistant to Roman Catholicism. We brought Jesuits with us, and they made a bloody botch of the religious training. They cut off fingers and ears when the Aztecs mispronounced the Latin words. To the Aztecs' credit, they gave Christianity a fair shake. They weren't resistant to the religion itself. In fact, they rather liked the idea of communion. And they found confession to be a droll experience, but that was probably because they had no concept of sin, and so they used the confessional to speak about crop failure and certain birds going extinct, digressions like that. But they wondered greatly that the Jesuits used the name of God so freely, when their own priests were forbidden to pronounce the name of their deity. If a God could be called so commonly, they argued, then what made it different from any other worldly thing? They proved to be shrewd theologians, those Aztec bankers, and they were downright picayune about consistency. They didn't want to hear about heresies or different forms of baptism or indulgences. They thought the whole idea of relics was a joke and laughed rather boisterously on that score, which prompted the practice of Jesuits cutting out Aztec tongues and vocal cords.

The Aztecs were quick to pick up languages, but they could never master nuance, idiomatic usage, and the like. For example, one day an exceptionally extroverted Aztec banker wandered into our camp and said he was hungry.

"*Quiero un perra caliente.*"

The mistake was an honest one. He thought he was saying: "I want a hot dog." But what he was really saving was "I want a bitch in heat."

Cortez shot him on the spot.

And, when the Aztec bankers finally figured out that we were actually robbing them, they did not attack us and they did not close the banks. What they did was to make sure that the tills were empty. Cortez could call them *basura* and *moscas* and *mocos* all he wanted, but the fact remained: There were no gems to rob. He could threaten the tellers all he wanted. The Aztec bankers believed in multiple afterlife, so dying was no more serious to them than bird-watching in the desert.

I began, in fact, to see their passive resistance as an incredibly effective weapon. Twenty of us were ruling twelve million of them by the strength of our hand-cannons, and the arithmetic was irrefutable. To waste an Aztec banker, we had to waste a bullet. In other words, each time we won, we lost.

Cortez went to ridiculous extremes to get maximum mileage out of every bullet. He lined Aztec bankers up in a row, one behind the other, and then he fired his hand-cannon point-blank into the stomach of the first. Sometimes, four or five Aztec bankers dropped from the same bullet, but as far as I could tell, this tactic was only staying the inevitable.

As a matter of revenge, I think, someone among the Aztecs coined a compound word for us. They called us *perruquadedos*, which means "wigged ones with hurtful fingers."

Cortez was livid. He made the Aztec bankers eat pork for breakfast. He insisted that Aztec children wear rosaries around their necks and say "*Vaya con Dios*" when they were leaving a room. And he laced the peyote with pesticides that the natives called *perruquat*, which means "wigged and hurtful drugs."

"Panza," he said to me one day, "*ven aquí*."

We huddled. Cortez wanted me to pretend disaffection, so

that I might go native. He wanted me to infiltrate the inner-most circles of the Aztec intelligentsia, so that he might know what made them tick.

This I did. I hired on at an Aztec bank at the minimum wage. I took to wearing white shirts and quoting Ambrose Bierce. It was my job to sweep the floors when there weren't any customers. This I did. Cortez wanted me to find out where they had hidden the rubies and emeralds, but I never found out.

What I did find out was most peculiar. The Aztecs, I discovered, do not know how much wealth they have, because they do not know about counting.* Their belief system is based on Oneness, and so their counting is in terms of that Oneness. For example, if there are two apples on a table, the Aztecs save "There are one more than one apple." They must repeat the one, no matter how many apples are on the table. And, if by chance there were two-hundred apples on the table, as happened one day, the result of a practical joke by Luis-Eduardo Fisher, a *bruto*, if ever there was one, the minds of the Aztecs would still not be blown. Montezuma, himself, came upon the two-hundred apples.

"*Manzana*," he said appreciatively.

The one substituted for the whole. I realized that Aztecs formed plurals by dropping the definite or indefinite article.

"*Manzana perrunuara*," Montezuma's daughter Connie said, meaning that the apples were probably poisoned.

The great Montezuma smiled. He didn't have to taste the apples to enjoy them. He was getting off on their Oneness.

By extension, then, since the Aztecs had no concept of counting, they had no sense of choices either. "Either-or" never occurred to them. Coming to a fork in the road and faced with a choice between two opposite paths, an Aztec would say "Always-also" and take both paths, one by the body, the other by the spirit.

---

* The Aztecs actually used a sophisticated counting system, based on the number twenty, not readily understood by European explorers.

I witnessed personally an even clearer example of the absence of choices in the Aztec mind. Cortez thought it would be good for my infiltration if he and the boys in the band robbed the bank in which I was working. That way, the Aztecs would know that he wasn't playing favorites.

So, they all came in one day, wearing red bandannas and brandishing pistolas and scimitars, shouting *basura* and *moscas* and *mocos*.

Cortez came up to me. I had been cleaning the empty tills and I put down my rag when I saw him.

"*¿Se habla español en este banco jodido?*" he asked.

"*La lingua franca,*" I said, trying to be cordial.

"*Alors,*" he said, "*Donnez-moi tous vos bijoux.*"

"*On est fauché,*" I said, holding up empty hands.

"*Fauché?*" he screamed. "*Fauché?*"

"*Que veux-tu qu'on y fasse?*"

Then Cortez went to the next till and confronted an Aztec banker.

"You got three choices, bean-picker," Cortez said. "You can gimme all your rubies and emeralds and kiss the sawdust off my boots. Or, two, you can take a bullet through the nose-hole and die. Or, three, you can pick a part of your body you want me to maim. What's it gonna be?"

I felt sorry for the young Aztec banker. He didn't understand the counting, and he had no concept of the choices involved. Cortez was thinking A, B or C, while the Aztec banker was thinking "Always-also."

As it turned out, Cortez didn't stick to any of the choices. He let Luis-Eduardo Fisher deviate the Aztec's septum with a pocket knife. And then Cortez ordered his men to fill their bags with stones and paperweights, things like that. He considered it bad form to let the Aztecs see him and his band of boys coming out of a bank with empty bags. Later that day, at the rendezvous point, which turned out to be the Trotsky Hotel, Cortez seemed excessively cheerful.

"Digame, Panza," he said, "how's that bean-picker doing?"

"He sleeps with the fishes," I said.

"No more *mocos*, eh?" Luis-Eduardo Fisher laughed, slopping more garbanzos on stale bread.

For the record, only half of the stories told about Cortez are true. It is true, for example, that we all wrote letters to the King, asking that he be recalled, while we were stationed in the Caribbean. It is also true that Cortez did not wait for any answer from the King and ordered that we set sail for Mexico immediately. He figured that he could buy back the King's favor with all the rubies and emeralds.

But it is not true that we went through the halls of Montezuma, past the zoo and banana trees, to hold that great Emperor hostage. Cortez and Montezuma played chess, and Cortez left Montezuma in a precarious position on the board, but that is not what I would call holding someone hostage.

It is true that Montezuma's daughter played a major role in interpreting for both sides. But it is not true that she deceived Cortez or that Cortez invoked the *droit du seigneur* and had his way with her. Connie Montezuma fell in love with me, and she and I were out in the desert, waiting for birds to fly overhead, even as the chess game was going on at the palace.

During the years of the Occupation, I became something of an expert on the vanquished Aztec culture. There is, of course, a fascination in all colonizing cultures, to know the cultures we decimate. The Aztecs call this "the law of pigs." Pork is taboo in their culture, and so many of their philosophical axioms have pork as a linchpin. Expressed in folkloric fable, as indeed all of their laws are, the law of pigs goes like this: There is a famine in an unnamed country, and a rather dumb farmer, who shall also go unnamed, decides that he must survive, and so he slaughters all his pigs, one by one. As he is killing the last pig, he realizes that he has indeed survived, but, in doing so, he has no farm animals left, and he is caught up with a curiosity akin to obsession about what it is like to be a pig, this last pig, for example, about to be slaughtered. But the farmer has eaten so much pork that he has become pig-like, and so he can never know, since one can never know oneself. In Spain we had no such folk tale. We simply said: "You are what you eat."

One day, an art appraiser came to Mexico City to evaluate the artefacts in Montezuma's city. He explained to me that "value" in art was determined by two things: the form of the piece and the material of the piece. And, since most objets d'art were made of gold, the material of the pieces was set, a constant variable, and so less interesting, according to Cordobal, the art appraiser. But the form could still be appraised, and that is why he came. He told me that objects sculpted to resemble farm animals, for example, were less valuable than birds and things that flew. The most cherished form was that of an eagle, with a snake in its mouth. I could only imagine his surprise, his shock and horror, to find out that we were melting everything down, birds, pigs and everything else in the art category, into gold bars.

"These ingots," he asked me, "do they have much value for you in your native land?"

"Oh, yes," I answered, "they're made of gold, which is very valuable."

I think he found my answer somewhat stupid, on the moron side of things, even pig-headed. But Cordobal was a patient man, and so he persisted.

"Yes, okay. We are agreed upon the value of gold. But are they valuable to you as ingots?"

"What do you mean?"

"The shape of the bars. The utter uniformity of the bars. Do you prize sameness in your art world?"

"No," I said. "We do that for shipping."

"I see," he said. "Do you not understand that these art objects are more valuable as pigs and archers and birds?"

"That may be so," I countered, "but our divine right kings have no interest in curios. If we melt them down, then our kings can see them for what they really are. Pure gold."

"Strange," Cordobal said. "An Aztec would place no value at all on these ingots, because they are all alike. You see, gold is of no value to us, if all it is is gold."

I had taken two art courses at the Prado in Madrid, and I have to say that I learned more about art in ten minutes with Cordobal than I did in two semesters at the Prado.

On another occasion, I happened to meet an Aztec geologist, looking at rock samples outside of Cuernevaca. He told me the best samples were found near volcanoes, those precious rocks that had been covered with lava. It didn't matter that the rock was gold or graphite underneath. What mattered was that the rock was covered with lava. These rocks had a religious significance for the Aztecs.

This geologist had an unpronounceable name. The closest translation I could find in Spanish nomenclature was Wenceslas. In talking with Señor Wenceslas, I discovered that science was synonymous with religion for the Aztecs, and further that he was a practiced shaman.

We got drunk together on a mountaintop, Wenceslas and I. It was on some cheap Dos Equis beer, as I recall. And, when he had mellowed out, Wenceslas told me the true translation of *chichimecas*. Now *chichimecas* is what we Spaniards sometimes called the Aztecs, and it was a pejorative term, meaning *dog-eaters*. Back home, we experienced explorers referred to the Italians the same way.

Lo and behold, I discovered that *chichimecas* did not mean *dog-eaters*, notwithstanding that one Aztec ordering *perra caliente*. It is a compound word, difficult to translate, and, as with all compound words in the Aztec language, deeply profound and better to think about than to say and bandy about. *Chichi*, of course, means *mother's milk*, without the lewd connotations of bared mammaries that we connote, but with the sacred sense of erupting volcanoes that the Aztecs connote. Mother's milk has always been considered a miracle by the Aztecs. It is, according to them, God's way of raining from within. We might say, somewhat unfeelingly, "When it rains, it pours." An Aztec would say, in the same situation: "God is flooding his children today." The *mecas* part is even more difficult to comprehend. It has to do with discipline, but of a special sort. It means self-flagellation, to be exact. In the Aztec religion, dualities dance. We might call it the merger of positive and negative energies. The Aztecs make no such value judgments, so, of course, they do not say *positive* or *negative*. When the two parts are put together, then, *chichimecas* means the merger of mother's milk and self-immolation. In other words, abundance tempered with punishment. Or: flooding with drought. Even as a mother expresses her milk, Wenceslas told me, her breasts are shrinking.

I began to see *chichimecas* as a metaphor for colonialism. Even as we expanded, we shrank. I am reminded that in voodoo cultures, shrunken heads symbolize one's largest enemies. It's the same principle, I think. And I began to realize that waiting for birds in the desert had as much to do with the presence of desert as with the absence of birds.

Rather than infiltrate the innermost circles of the Aztec intelligentsia, I would say that what happened was that the Aztec spirit invaded me. I began doing peyote with Connie Montezuma, and I found the spiritual peace that had eluded me throughout my life. We conceived a son together, which means that we had to have sex at some point, but I do not honestly recall ever having penetrated Connie Montezuma. The spirit world is a powerful place.

Cortez, of course, thought I had betrayed him, and he promised that he would castrate me personally before he left the country.

Things went badly for Cortez in the latter years of his stay in Mexico. Pizarro had cleaned up on the Incas in Peru and was already back in Europe, getting large crowds and dowry wherever he went. His triumphant return to Europe also meant that Cortez had lost the wager. Apparently, if Cortez had won, he would have gotten his way with Pizarro's sister. And, because Pizarro won, he was able to lay claim to Felicia, the very surprised sister of Cortez. As it turned out, the joke was doubly on poor Hernando, because Pizarro didn't have a sister, but only a younger brother, a rather doltish lad named Ozzie.

Then Cortez contracted gout, and his legs enlarged so badly that he couldn't get in and out of Aztec banks, whose doors were constructed for very tall, very thin people. And so it was that Aztec bankers lost all fear of him. He became a *passe-mot*, a kind of town joke to them.

Whenever they heard him outside the bank, shouting *basura* and pulling in his stomach for an attempted entry in profile, they would look up at one another and either laugh or wink, calling him *canepilotus*, which means "wigged duck-waddle with spaz fingers."

By the time Cortez left Mexico, he was in no shape to castrate anybody. They had to hoist him onto the ship by means of a pulley, because stretchers had not yet been invented.

I had family obligations in Mexico, and so, of course, I stayed on. I still don't know what the Aztecs did with all the rubies and emeralds, but Connie Montezuma winks at me when we are in the desert, and I think the secret must have something to do with the increasing rarity of migrating birds.

The Inquisition of Erasmus

*In his middle years Hernando Cortez wondered if it might not be better to have discovered and died than to have colonized and then come back to a life of slow oblivion. The king and queen were displeased with the way he had conducted himself in the Aztec occupation. And yet he was a world-class explorer, a fact which could not be denied. Deference was shown to him. Civil courtesies were strictly observed. His name still figured on the guest list of parties at court. But he was an explorer who did no exploring. He was given the title of "emeritus," but no new ships.

He sat in the Plaza de Segovia, the middle of Madrid on an August afternoon, sipping cognac and anisette with Balboa at the Club de Conquistadores. The combination of heat, humidity, idleness, gout and this drink that the Spanish called *sol y sombra*, sunshine and shade, gave him a heady buzz, a dreamy wistfulness, which he shared with the doltish Balboa.

"Do you ever miss it, Bo?"

"What is it, Hernando?" Balboa asked, his words twittering, his lips shimmering like the bulls at Pamplona.

"World-class exploring."

"*¡Ay que te lleva la chingada!*" Balboa said, cursing in what he imagined to be a coarse Mexican accent he had affected to impress his friends.

Cortez waited for a saner response.

"Naw," Balboa said, "that was all a bunch of ships and diarrhea, that life. Ships and diarrhea. You list this way, you list that way. You fight with pirates. You dream about mermaids. Pretty soon you don't recognize a woman if she doesn't look too slippery, you know? I got tired of eating fish and having diarrhea. And all those dingy tars, you know? They stink up a ship and go potty wherever they feel like it. Like renters. They don't take pride in their vessel. And they tell the same Portuguese jokes, voyage after voyage, you know? Like, how can you tell the bride at a Portuguese wedding? She's the only one with curlers under her arms. I heard that one on six straight crossings."

"But you discovered Panama. Doesn't that mean something to you?"

"¡*Pinche Panama!*" Balboa said. "Is one big sand dune, Panama. Is not a continent. Is in between. I go halfway round the world to discover an in-between place. If all I wanted was a canal, I could have gone to Amsterdam. Or Venice. They got canals. You know the only good thing to come out of Panama?"

"No. What?"

"That saying: 'A man, a plan, a canal—Panama.' Is the same if you say it backwards or forwards. I think maybe the Portuguese made it up, as revenge for all those jokes."

"I have regrets."

"The Aztecs weren't as rich as the Incas. Is a big regret, no?"

"No, I'm not talking about material gain."

"What other kind of gain is there?"

"I have . . . "

"Jes . . . ?"

"I have nostalgia for the infinite."

"What is this *cucaracha*? This is like saying you have pockets full of rye. It doesn't mean anything."

"You are a baobab, Bo. A real baobab."

Outside the Club de Conquistadores, the children were playing tag with death's-head moth masks and singing.

"The world is flat
The world is round,
The world is neither
Under the ground. "

＊

Mid-life crisis befell Cortez like a compound fracture: the same echoed urgency of snap, crackle and pop. He had seen other explorers go sour at the bib. He had witnessed their agoraphobia, their whining narcissism, the dyslexia in their penmanship. And more: their hurried decisions, their enanteodromia into other philosophies and religions, wasted energies at pi, long depressions like *calamares en su tinto.* Their wistful wanton ways. He could have fallen back on his gout, spending his pension and his days sipping *sol y sombra* with high-tide bores like Balboa. He could retire to the country and quill his memoirs. Or he could go on the speaker circuit, like Magellan, De Soto, Jacques Cartier and Henry Hudson. He could even hire out to pirates, since he knew all the major explorers' routes. But no. He did not want to go especially gentle into that *buena noche.*

So he went to Barcelona and hired on with a whaling ship called the Punto de Vista. Its captain, an English greaser named Downey, was a coffee addict, bent on riding bareback on a great white whale. He wore a red bandanna, talked about harpoons a lot, and said a friend of his, a bloater named McGee, swam into the afterlife on the back of a whale.

Downey had his druthers about who crewed and who didn't. He had no inclination for exploring or explorers, so Cortez told him that he was a geographer and linguist. Downey was too high on java to care, one way or the other.

"Geography is nice."

"And necessary," Cortez said, feeling that he was being patronized.

"I bet we still get lost," Downey laughed, tossing doubloons underhanded, like horseshoes, into a spittoon.

Three months later, lost somewhere near Tuli, Greenland, they spotted a gam of humpback whales. Wearing fresh buckskins, Downey tried to ride one to his death, but the whale bucked him, and the crew had to fish him out, unceremoniously, like a drunk.

Still, the kill was three whales, so everybody worked and everybody ate well.

Then a Japanese whaler approached them. Their captain cupped his hands and hollered.

"*Anatano blubberwa, totemo oishii desuka?*"

"What's he saying?" Downey asked Cortez.

"I think he's saying we'd better get out of his territorial waters."

"Okay, men," Downey said, shaking himself like a wet dog, "prepare to fire."

Downey's reaction to any other ship he encountered was to blow it out of the water.

"Remember, boys," he said, "to baptize them as you're taking aim."

And then he looked around for Quintero, his best whaler.

"Quintero, I want you to take out the captain. With a harpoon. Above the belt, if possible. I want to troll with him behind the boat. He might attract some whales."

It was done as he had commanded. The Japanese sailors were slaughtered with muskets and cannons and crossbows, while Quintero aced the captain with a harpoon in the stomach and ripped him off the deck of his ship, to dangle at the end of the line behind the whaling boat. The captain proved to be excellent bait, not only for whales, but also for sharks, grouper and barracuda.

And, when only the lower intestines remained on the end of the barb, Downey blessed that captain again, and Quintero crossed himself, saying, *"La tripa del santo."*

But then fishing with human bait proved so successful that Downey began harpooning his own tars as they slept or swabbed the deck and trolling them behind the boat. As long as the fishing was good, nobody complained about the diminishing numbers of the crew.

"Pescado y paño," Quintero said, crossing himself again and proclaiming the miracle of the fishes and the loaves.

Cortez knew that a geographer-linguist was too nonessential a job on the Punto de Vista, and so he jumped ship when they docked in Newfoundland.

In the streets of Halifax the children sang.

> *"Le monde est plat,*
> *Le monde est rond,*
> *Le monde en bas*
> *Est si profond."*

✳

After a year of feeling eclipsed by his own shadow, with numerous nightmares of Aztec corpses burning on a funeral pyre, Cortez resolved to devote the next three years to finding and deciphering the meaning of life.

He decided to go ask royalty, since they were supposed to have a divine right to know a thing like that.

He went to Granada, where he interviewed Boabdil, the last Moorish King of Granada, just before the latter's beheading.

"What is the meaning of life?" Cortez asked.

"You are a sot and a Christian. Why should I answer you?"

"Because my mind is open."

Boabdil was not convinced. He had never met a Christian with an open mind.

"My children shall feast on your children, vital organ by vital organ," he said defiantly. "My people shall reclaim this land, inch'allah by inch'allah."

"Tomorrow you will lose your head," Cortez said, "and they will baptize you. At the moment of your death, you will become a saint. Would you care to comment on that?"

"Yes," Boabdil said. "Why is martyrdom required to become a saint?"

"I don't honestly know," Cortez said. "But it's easier than working three miracles. They're asking me to leave. Please tell me what, in your estimation, is the meaning of life?"

"Read my lips tomorrow."

Cortez attended the beheading. When the axe fell and the head of St. Boabdil rolled off the block and into the bushel basket, the lips were moving. They seemed to be saying one thing: *Mentira.*

Cortez went to Italy and interviewed Cesare Borgia, who was in-between Popes.

"What is the meaning of life?" Cortez asked.

"Indulgence," Borgia answered, without hesitation.

"You mean, tolerance?"

"No, indulgence."

"Self-indulgence?"

"Others'."

"I don't understand."

"What's to understand? You sell them through the Church."

Cortez attended a roundelay at the court of Duc Charles de Bourbon, who was the Constable of France.

"What is the meaning of life, your Duke?" Cortez asked.

"*Vous osez me provoquer avec ces mots,*" Duc Charles answered, dipping his fingers in his wine goblet for good measure.

"I simply must ask them," Cortez said.

"A healthy liver, then."

Cortez was still not satisfied. He voyaged far and wide to the throne of Muhammad Babar, who was laying plans for a Mogul Dynasty in India.

"Muhammad Babar, what is the meaning of life?"

"I like these big questions," Babar said, stroking his chin as though it were a fetish. "You see," he grinned, speaking with pointillist diction, "this question has been asked by pundits and Punjabi alike, and it is not multiple choice, as you say in the West. It is a correct question with a correct answer. But, to arrive at the one correct answer, you must first become an apprentice to all who are holy and know. You must curry their favor, and when you are old and alone, dying from some impeccable disease, then you must curry some more."

Cortez continued his Asian swing and went surreptitiously, in the disguise of a prince chasing fireflies, to the Tatami kingdom of the Iyeyasu clan in Kyoto, who were then laying plans for the Tokugawa shogunate. He noted that the Japanese practiced crucifixions, without being Christians. They pronounced every syllable, just like the Castellanos. They ate *calimares en su tinto*, and the Portuguese rumor back home was false: They did not eat boiled dog. What Cortez especially liked about the Japanese was that they revered explorers, seeing them as ghost spirits or gods.

Cortez attended a Noh play near Lake Hakkone and thought he understood the meaning of life: Move very slowly, be mostly silent, and do your duty. A Zen master clarified these lessons for him.

"If a mortal lifts but one foot, he cannot then lift the other foot. The principle of roots. And, if a mortal hears two songbirds singing at once, he cannot hear them separately. The principle of synchronicity. And, if a mortal sees everything out of one eye, he still cannot see everything, because one eye cannot see the other eye. The principle of double vision. And the most valuable fruits fall to the least descrying hands."

So saying, he gave Cortez a lotus blossom and a lily pad, and he bade him farewell.

Cortez continued on his eastward path, trusting in blind faith, slow movements and lots of silence for his navigational principles. He saw natives eating each other in the Fiji Islands. He witnessed absurd sexual practices in Samoa, like twin-swapping, incest-adulation, chicken-coupling and risque limericks. In Hawaii he saw his first volcano, which the natives swore spoke the word of God, but in "lava language that nobody listens to." In Baja, California, he found Alonso de Alvarade, drunk and working as a caterer for a group of matriarchal Hopi Indians, whose motto was: "She who laughs, lasts." Alvarado was one of those rare men who had served under both Cortez in Mexico and Pizarro in Peru. He was an expert traveler, an affable storyteller, and multilingual. When Cortez found him, Alvarado was giddy with raucous laughter, professing that laughter itself was the one thing that neither kings nor popes could control.

At gunpoint, Cortez persuaded Alvarado to set sail with him for Peru. There they met Huáscar, the famous Inca prince, who was more kindly disposed toward Cortez than Montezuma had been.

"What is the meaning of life?" Cortez asked him.

"There is no meaning," Huáscar said. "That is how we have endured your domination."

Outside Huáscar's palace, the Inca children were dancing in a circle and singing.

> *"El mundo es triste,*
> *El mundo es chiste,*
> *Por dónde vaya*
> *La vida es maya. "*

*

Having struck out with royalty, Cortez went back to Spain, his pockets full of gold ingots from Peru, but his heart still empty of answers.

He decided to ask the artists next.

He went to England and asked to speak with that country's greatest writer. They sent him to Miles Coverdale, a noted Bible translator.

"What is the meaning of life?" Cortez asked.

"To translate is to betray," Coverdale said. "Leastways, that's what them good-buddy Italianos say."

"Why do you do it?"

"The word of God? Why not? I'd rather fail at the primo prize in life than win a cooking contest. Know what I mean?"

"You talk strangely, Miles. Where do you come from? Sheffield? Leeds?"

"Nossir. I'm a country boy, myself."

"And you're qualified to translate the Bible?"

"I don't cotton to splitting no angels on the head of a pin, if that's what you mean. Who you got doing the Spanish translations?"

"I don't honestly know."

"Well? There you have it. It's a tough job, but some-body's gotta do it. I'm in Leviticus right now. You care to parse a few paragraphs with me?"

"Thanks, no. I have to be going."

"Then go with the Big One shining down on you."

Cortez went to Holland next, where he met with Gerard David, the Dutch painter, and Josquin Des Prez, the famous contrapuntist.

"What is the meaning of life?" he asked them.

The two got into such a terrible row over semantics that Cortez had to leave, without an answer.

He went to France next, where he had interviews with

Joachim Du Bellay and Clement Marot, both of whom thought he was trying to steal their poems. Du Bellay may have been light in his verses, but he was stuffy and overbearing in life. He said no weasel-eyed Spaniard was going to get any answers from him, and he would challenge Cortez to a duel before he would endure any Mediterranean cheek. Marot said pretty much the same thing, with less aplomb.

That left Italy, the boot of Europe, which reminded Cortez of several axioms: "If the cap has a question, let the boot answer it." And: "Boots, boots, the feet have no roots." Or: "If the boot fits, it soon will be stolen."

Cortez went to interview Correggio, the Florentine painter of frescoes. He went to Correggio, because he was fascinated with a painter whose name meant *correction*. His real name was Antonio Allegri, but he was anything but happy. Cortez found him on a scaffold in Parma, painting the dome of a church. Cortez was at once impressed and astonished by the intense emotional feeling in Correggio's painting and the complex configurations of clouds, which created the illusion of a church ceiling opening onto sky.

"You are subtle, like a puppy," Cortez said, complimenting Correggio for the latter's soft treatment of human flesh, making women's cheeks look like spoiled peaches. "You have a strong, even harsh command of gentle light, and a delicate, even staccato sense of shading."

"Light and shade, light and shade," Correggio muttered, coming down from his ladder. "Do you believe, sir, that I have succeeded in creating the illusion of an open sky up there?"

"Yes, I would say yes."

"Ah, but the test, sir, is with birds, not people."

Correggio took two turtledoves out of a cage.

"Thus far, these birds have refused to fly, precisely because they know there is paint up there. Let us see if they can be fooled today."

He let go of the two birds, and they immediately made for

the configuration of cumulus clouds on the dome, crashing their heads into the dome and falling, errant feathers and all, to their deaths below.

Correggio baptized them and put them into a burlap bag.

"God, I feel great," he said, and then he stopped and pondered for a moment. "Do you really think they have souls?"

"I don't know about that," Cortez said.

"This is a country in which all the holy people talk to birds. Francis of Assisi, Anthony of Padua, all the instant-halo people. I wouldn't want it getting around that two doves met their deaths because of my frescoes."

"I will go to the grave with your secret," Cortez promised.

"Good. That's what I wanted to hear. I'll introduce you to a living saint for your promise. Her name is Saint Angela Merici. She founded the Ursuline Order of nuns. Everybody wants to sleep with her, but she's a living saint, you know, and so they can't. America was named after her. Did you know that? It was definitely *not* named after Amerigo Vespucci, but after Saint Angela Merici. Only she didn't want anything as big as a continent named after her, so she lets on that it's Amerigo's claim to fame. This is a great day for me. We'll invite Saint Angela for supper. You'll see."

Apparently, Correggio saw Cortez as a good omen, that his arrival had something to do with finally being able to deceive the doves. Cortez was not about to dissuade him from this belief. It was an auspicious beginning, and he meant to capitalize on it.

"Tony, I've been around the world several times, asking everybody the same question. Now I've come to you. What is the meaning of life?"

"I suffer in the shadow of Andrea del Sarto and that cuisinartist, Leo da Vinci. Everybody asks da Vinci that question. You see, he's not only a painter and sculptor. He's an architect and an engineer. He puts on a modest face and says he dabbles, and what would a dabbler know? Makes me sick, that sort of modesty. All the while, I'm twice as spiritual, and I get his leftover interviews. Did you go to him first?"

"No, I came straightway to you."

"God, I like you better and better. What was your question again?"

"What is the meaning of life?"

"Arguably, a tough question. Hmmm. Well, it seems to me it's a matter of distinguishing between figure and ground, between that which is enclosed and that which is not. There is gravity, of course, which is body-based, but that doesn't explain perspective nor our perceptions of perspective. Do you think anyone has ever asked that question from a completely primitive state, which is to say, without any preconceptions or bias at all? Like asking, what is a straight line in nature? What is an angle? What is a period? A *mise-en-abime*? You see, I have rephrased your question, in terms of optics. I have given you parallel questions, which amount, finally and in a phenomenological sense, to the same thing. What, then, *is* the meaning of life? I think it is singularly instructive that I have succeeded in convincing two turtledoves that the dome of this church was the same as the open sky on a clear or semi-clear day. If that illusion is possible, and you are my witness that it is, then it must mitigate any empirical answer I might give to your question. Do you see?"

"Frankly, no."

"Repeat your question."

"What is the meaning of life?"

"I don't know."

They had supper with Saint Angela Merici, an excellent veal, as it turned out. She wore a halo, which, after several attempts to disprove its existence, Cortez had to admit was real. When the sun went down, Correggio didn't have to bother with candles. They supped by the light of Saint Angela's halo.

Cortez thought that she was an incredibly beautiful woman. After four glasses of wine, he found himself saying so.

"I have to admit, Saint Angela . . . "

"Call me Angie."

"I have to admit, Saint Angie, that I am quite taken by you."

"And I by you, Spaniard. I have always had a soft spot for fellows of the truly Latin persuasion."

It turned out that her idol was Odoacer, who was the first barbarian king to rule the Roman Empire, after its collapse.

"I find pagans frightfully attractive," she said.

"May I ask you a question?"

"Of course."

"What, in your holy estimation, is the meaning of life?"

"I think it depends upon what one has never experienced. We always tend to think in terms of what has evaded our senses, exceeded our grasp, or estranged us with its otherness."

"Is this your answer?"

"No. It's the qualification, without which my answer would be absurd. Repeat your question."

These Italians had a fondness for having questions repeated.

"What is the meaning of life?" he repeated.

"Orgasm," she said, without batting an eyelash, and it seemed to Cortez that, for a moment at least, her halo was on fire.

✻

Having strived, nay, striven these many years for an answer to the question, "What is the meaning of life?," Cortez decided to give up. Having searched high and low these many years for an answer, he decided to give up. He did not want his old age cluttered with such a question. He was even beginning to salt, pepper and otherwise season his conversation with vague inanities like "these many years," and he didn't like it.

It was so easy to be mediocre. Kings and princes, poets and saints, all of them were chiseled on the cutting edge of mediocrity. Their mediocrity echoed in him like an abscessed tooth.

So it was that Balboa complained of a toothache, as they sipped *sol y sombra* on the Plaza de Segovia at the Club de Conquistadores.

"You are drunk, Bo. Let's go to the bulls."

"*Vámonos*," Balboa concurred.

"I like you, Bo," Cortez said. "You are so middle gray."

"You've been talking like a painter ever since you got back from Italy."

They went to the *corrida*, and Cortez watched the bulls go charging to their stupid deaths, one after another. He was about to contemplate suicide when he saw Saint Ignatius of Loyola blessing the severed ear of one of the bulls. Ignatius was a saint, everybody knew he was a saint, he even said he was a saint, but, contrary to Saint Angela Merici, Ignatius did not have a halo. Or, if he had one, he never wore it in public.

He was a founder. His forte was founding things. The Society of Jesus, the Fraternal Order of Jesuits and Jesuettes, Opus Dei, Agnus Dei, the Lavatory at Pompeii and Bulls for Jesus, he had founded all of them. In addition, he was known far and wide to be a world-class Inquisitioner.

Cortez asked him, in the middle of that bloodthirsty throng, what, in his estimation, the meaning of life was. Loyola recognized him immediately, for, as a teenager, Loyola had dreamed of being a world-class explorer, and not a Jesuit priest.

"I would just love to hear your confession," he bubbled. "I would dearly love it."

The next day, then, Cortez went to confession at the Cathedral.

"I have had arrogant thoughts," Cortez began, "and even unruly ambitions."

"Cut the shimmy," Loyola said. "You've killed Aztecs."

"Yes, I have," Cortez began, "but I baptized each and every one of them in blood."

"That's very good, then. What about women?"

"What about them?"

"You've been around the world, my friend. Did you indulge in strange and exotic practices? Did you do them in bizarre and perverse positions, other than the missionary? Come on now. Did ya? Did ya?"

"Here and there, I tarried and dallied."

"I want numbers. Names and numbers and an exact accounting. I need to know, uh, for the sake of giving you your penance. Everything. Blow by blow."

After four hours, they were finished. Cortez felt spent. Loyola, too, seemed to have a flushed face, but he did not look spent.

"I've never had such a thorough confession, Ignazio."

"I'd like to do that again sometime," Loyola said, with a wistful, wanton look on his face.

"What is the meaning of life?" Cortez said bluntly.

"For that, you must go on a pilgrimage."

"Another trip?"

"You're used to it. It'll be a snap. Besides, you're going with me."

"Where, may I ask?"

"The Netherlands. I'm going to inquisition Erasmus. You can come along and watch. Besides, it's one of my stock questions when I inquisition."

✳

Cortez had nothing better to do, so he went along. They stayed one night in Basque country, and Loyola complained that the people who lived in border territories were usually pagan, political and rooted to the land, not to the heavens.

"You can't teach a Basque to make a leap of faith. He simply will not leap. He's interested in relics, but only of the most provincial sort. And he's not interested in indulgences at all. Give him good crops and he'll worship you. But he will never obey a pope in Rome or a king in Madrid."

Loyola had to stop talking, so that he could whip himself for an hour. Cortez watched, astonished. When he was full of bloody welts, Loyola stopped.

"There are some places on my back I can't get to. Would you mind?"

He was offering the whip to Cortez.

"I don't think I could. Really."

"Come on. It's simple."

"I've never whipped a priest before."

"You ought to try it on yourself sometime. You would see how much closer to the narrow path you would be, and then it would be no problem for you to come to the aid of a fellow Christian."

In Paris they were met by a cortège of clerics, all Loyalists, who wanted to show the Grand Inquisitioner their body welts and get his blessing. Loyola was pleased by this group display. He took it as a sign that the word of God was spreading, like margarine, over the entire extinct Holy Roman Empire.

"Do you see, Hernando?" Loyola said, standing up in their carriage and waving to the populace, his fingers replicating those of the elderly popes when they bless at the Basilica. "Wheat and chaff alike, people are taking to the streets and whipping themselves. Such public displays cannot fail to attract the attention of Jesus Christ, our Lord and Savior, who was, himself, whipped pretty good."

Cortez was familiar with the practice of giving forty lashes to insubordinate tars, but he had never attached any religious significance to this practice.

"Tell me about Erasmus."

"Desiderius Erasmus."

"Yes?"

"He's a priest. And a wondrous Bible translator. His translations into Greek and Latin are ground-breaking works. But then Martin Luther is a priest as well, and his translation of the Bible into German is also a masterpiece. I wonder, what is it with these priests who translate the Bible? What makes them become Reformers?"

Cortez was intensely curious now. A priest whose name meant Desire. Father Desire. How coolly concupiscent.

"Have you inquisitioned Martin Luther, Iggy?"

"Too late. He broke from the corral already. Excommunicated. I hear he's sorry now. Sent him off the deep end. I hear from my spies that he sits alone in a hair shirt, brooding, sticking pins in his skin, trying to write Christmas carols. But Erasmus is more cunning. He's stayed within the Church. He's known as a wit, you know? You can get away with saying the most horrible things, if you say them with humor. Comedy has always been the least censored of the arts. But we'll get him on the rack and see if he still makes jokes then."

"Have you ever made a mistake, Iggy? I mean, is it possible to torture a Saint?"

"Absolutely, in which case I have only sped up his sainthood. Every martyr needs a hatchet man, you know? Where would Moses have been, without the pharaoh running interference for him? Even Jesus, himself, needed a Judas, to look even better. It is quite probable that Erasmus is a saint, just like I am. If so, all the more sanctifying this experience will be for both of us. Two saints never made a devil, you know."

Cortez studied the brief on Erasmus, while Loyola whipped himself in the outer rooms of the Inn outside Rotterdam, where Erasmus was born.

Father Desire was the foremost Christian humanist of the whole Renaissance. A classics major. Greek and Latin stylist. (Leave it to the Dutch, to speak anything but Dutch, Cortez thought.) Studied in Paris. Went to England, where he became friends with Sir Thomas More. There was a note on More and the apparent need for an inquisition on him at some later date. Apparently, it was More's humor that first charmed Erasmus into exploring his own wit. Came back to Holland. Less travel, more writing. In books like *Adagia* and *Praise of Folly*, Erasmus satirized the clergy, accusing them of ignorance with witticisms, like calling them "priests of burden" and making rhymes like "Mass" and "ass." He accused the clerics of failing to educate the masses. (No rhyme in the plural, Cortez thought.) Erasmus accused his fellow priests of not practicing charity, of not studying the Bible, of selling indulgences, of creating imaginary saints for the purpose of selling their relics.

And yet, even in the brief that Cortez read, there were quotes attributed to Erasmus that clearly showed that Erasmus cared about the unity of Christianity, did not wish to follow in Luther's footsteps, was even willing to recant everything if the Church could be bettered by his doing so.

The more he read, the more Cortez liked this Desiderius Erasmus, whose nickname was Geert. Cortez was sure, without ever having met the man, that Erasmus was an enlightened being, a smart and humble fellow, one who was blessed with bliss beyond his years and cursed by a Catholicism that was behind the times.

When they arrived at the Great Hall in The Hague, Erasmus was waiting for them, stripped to his long underwear, his hands and feet in chains.

"I would shake your hand if I could," Erasmus said when he was introduced to Cortez.

"Free him," Loyola commanded, and it was done. "I must tell you, Father Erasmus," Loyola said, scanning the man with the scrutiny of a farmer about to slaughter his pig, "that I can see auras. Your aura is most impressive. It threatens to break out as a halo on the visible plane at any moment."

"Thank you for your confidence," Erasmus said. "Your reputation precedes you, as always, Your Eminence."

Erasmus had a decidedly dry wit, long thin lips that always grinned but rarely smiled, like the British. He had high arching eyebrows that turned his every stare into a test of irony.

"It will be my pleasure to torture you," Loyola said.

And they set in to long discourses on theology. The more abstract Loyola tried to be, the more puns Erasmus made. The former kept insisting on blind faith and whippings. The latter kept insisting on charity, good works and a sense of humor. They had, it seemed to Cortez, irreconcilable differences.

In the spectators' gallery, Cortez was not alone.

"We meet again, good buddy."

Cortez recognized immediately the country drawl of Miles Coverdale.

"What are you doing here, Miles?"

"I got what ya'd call a vested interest here. Y'all may not be big on Bible translating in Spain, but up North it's big. Well sir, Luther, he was a good'un, but now he done got hisself excommunicated. And now, iffen ole 'Rasmus here gets thrown out on his cassock or martyred or such, well, that would leave a lot of reputation left for yours truly. I might even get to be official Bible scholar down to Rome."

"I see what you mean."

Cortez perked up his ears when he heard Loyola say to Erasmus, "What is the meaning of life?" Unfortunately, the answer came in Greek with, according to Miles Coverdale, two bilingual puns.

Loyola had Erasmus' knuckles broken, and then the proceedings moved outdoors, since the weather was clement, to the apple orchard, where Erasmus was tortured in the orchard. He was tied by his feet and left to dangle upside down, while Loyola threatened to swing him like a pendulum and then turn him into a human pretzel if he didn't recant. Of course, Erasmus recanted immediately, but Loyola pretended not to hear. He had not come all this way to get such quick contrition from a contortionist like Erasmus.

"Who is thy master?" Loyola demanded.

"The same as thine."

"Nonsense. You see things in reverse."

"*Honi soit qui bien y pense.*"

"*Carthago delenda est.*"

"The periphrastic!"

"Indeed. How many angels on the head of a pin?"

"Safety or bobby?"

"What was the correct answer to the riddle of the Sphinx?"

"Man."

"What is the most sanctifying sacrament?"

"The Eucharist."

"The least?"

"Extreme unction."

"What is the worst sin?"

"Pride."

"Who discovered America?"

"Opinion varies."

"After whom was America named?"

"Saint Angela Merici."

"Where do babies go when they haven't been baptized?"

"Limbo."

"Is it a nice place?"

"It has all the creature comforts. It lacks only the sight of the divine."

"Is the Pope infallible?"

"In matters of faith."

"What do you think of indulgences?"

"Depends."

"Upon what?"

"Upon whom they indulge."

"And relics?"

"Like obscenities. They cannot hurt a good soul. They will not help a bad one."

"What do you think of Martin Luther?"

"A brilliant man."

"And?"

"A great writer."

"And?"

"A spirit to be reckoned with."

"But he ridiculed you in *The Bondage of the Will*."

"He's not the first. Nor, apparently, the last."

"He argues that salvation is a gift from God. One cannot do anything to earn it. He ridiculed your belief in charity and good works."

"He has his opinion."

"Have you read his book?"

"Yes."

"Have you read any of my books?"

"No."

"Pity," Loyola said, turning to his aides-de-camp. "Cut him down. We'll begin anew tomorrow after matins."

They cleared the orchard, until only a few stunned spectators remained.

"Who are these people?" Cortez asked Miles Coverdale.

"Well, those two over yonder, they's Nicholas Ridley and Michael Servetus. Both theologs, both would-be martyrs.

That wild boar over there, that's John of Leiden. He's a Dutch Anabaptist fanatic. They say he eats his shoes for penance. And the dapper gent behind him, that's Ulrich von Hutten. He's one of Luther's spies. Whenever anyone talks, Hutten listens."

"And who are those wet people behind the peach trees?"

"They's devotees of Jan Hus. They soak themselves in petrol. If the inquisitioner mentions the name of Jan Hus, they set themselves on fire. If he doesn't, they go home, disillusioned. They's regulars at these proceedings."

"A strange and motley crew, all," Cortez mused.

"Frankly, I expected more royalty myself," Miles said. "Well, I'm off to work on Galatians. Hasta manzana," he quipped.

Loyola approached and asked Cortez if he had enjoyed the proceedings. It seemed to Cortez a funny word to use. Then, Loyola announced that he would have to sequester himself for the duration of the inquisition, and he hoped that Cortez could manage on his own for a few days.

What Cortez did, after supping on blood-squalor soup, braised beef tips, baby onions and baked beans, was to go to the cell of Erasmus. To his surprise, Cortez was neither frisked nor questioned. Apparently, everyone knew that he had come with Loyola, and so he was allowed to enter the penitent's cell without impediment.

"How are you holding up, Erasmus?"

"Who wishes to know?"

"I come of my own free will."

"There's a theological debate in what you say, but we shall let it pass. I ache, Hernando, to answer your query."

"May I call you Geert?"

"Why would you want to do that?"

"I feel that I know you. I admire you. I wish this cup could pass away from you."

"Don't get too blasphemous, son. The walls have ears. And you'd best curb your admiration before your countryman ties you to the apple tree. At least, he didn't shake the tree, huh?"

"Geert, may I be frank with you?"

"Why not?"

"What is the meaning of life?"

"Are you earnest or do you jest?"

"I am earnest."

"You are a refreshing simp, my son, I dare say."

"I said I am earnest, Geert."

"Do you want the Church answer?"

"Which is?"

"To know, love and serve God, in this world and in the next."

"Are there any other answers?"

"I have a personal one."

"May I have that one?"

"Find work that is play for you and help others. That is the meaning of my life."

"It's a better answer than any I've gotten so far," Cortez said.

"It doesn't come to many of us in dramatic fashion," Erasmus said. "Like Saul on the road to Damascus. Or Martin Luther's thunderstorm."

"Well, I'm retired from exploring, so I guess I don't have to worry about turning work into play."

"On the contrary. You have to worry more than most. You see, for most people, living gets to be hard work when they don't have their work anymore. You have to turn living into play. And, then, of course, you have to help others."

"For salvation?"

"For the hell of it."

"Maybe I could help you out of your predicament?"

"You have influence over the inquisitioner?"

"He likes my confessions."

"I can't ask you to do that. On the other hand, I wouldn't stop you either."

So it was that Cortez sent a message to Loyola, pleading with him for an end to the inquisition of Erasmus. Further, Cortez suggested an ecumenical council of all the great minds of Europe: Correggio, Da Vinci, Erasmus, Thomas More, even Martin Luther, in a nonvoting *ex officio* capacity.

The answer came back in three hours.

Querido Hernando:

What you suggest is both heretical and wise. You are a deep thinker, with visions that will take centuries to realize. The council you suggest is not feasible. The pardoning of Erasmus that you suggest is possible. However, I need to have a few more days with him, so that the Church does not lose face in this matter. Thanking you in advance for your concern, I am

Yours at the whip,

Ignazio

The next day, Loyola stretched Erasmus on the giant wheel and rode him to market and back. Children were encouraged to throw stones at Erasmus, but, of course, they didn't.

The interrogation consisted of a series of story problems that had to do with ethics and snap judgments.

Loyola: It's your birthday. You are given a calfskin wallet.

Erasmus: I wouldn't take it.

Loyola: You have a little boy. He comes to you with a butterfly, plus the killing jar.

Erasmus: I am not permitted by my vows to have a little boy.

Loyola: You are watching an execution. Suddenly, you notice a wasp on your arm.

Erasmus: I would bless it, in Jesus' name.

Loyola: You are watching a stage play. Afterwards, there is a banquet. Appetizer of raw oysters. Entree of boiled dog.

Erasmus: I would talk discreetly about the stage play and mind my table manners.

Loyola: You are on a desert island with a naked woman.

Erasmus: I would swim all day around the island, averting my eyes all the while.

Loyola: The naked woman calls to you for help.

Erasmus: I would inquire into the nature of her predicament, all the while averting my eyes.

Loyola: The naked woman is a nun. It might be Saint Angela Merici.

Erasmus: In that case, I would consider the situation to be in God's hands, and I would swim to shore to be of service.

Loyola: You are asked to rank the Jesuits, the Franciscans and the Dominicans. In what order would you rank them?

Erasmus: In the order prescribed by my superiors, all the way up to Our Holy Father in Rome.
 Etc.

  Cortez spent that entire night awake and alone, fasting and praying for forgiveness. It seemed to him a colossal injustice that Desire Erasmus should go on trial for having edified the poor with instruction and alms, while he, Cortez, had slaughtered so many Aztecs and was, nonetheless, allowed to sit as a privileged spectator at these manic proceedings. By early morning, he was given to hallucinations.

The morning of that third day began in a most dramatic fashion. Erasmus was stripped and whipped without breakfast. Then, he was stretched on the rack. Then, his head was tonsured, and eggs were broken on his bald spot. The spirit of Erasmus flagged visibly.

Miles Coverdale swooned in ecstasy and had to be carried out of the Great Hall.

John of Leiden began reciting the Scriptures backwards, forcing rhymes in clang association, and he, too, had to be removed from the Great Hall.

Nicholas Ridley and Michael Servetus began chanting the Lives of the Saints, especially those that had ended in the most garish displays of bloodshed, and they were not able to continue in the Great Hall.

The followers of Jan Hus looked especially wet that morning, and they began to shimmer and glow with gasoline. When one of them produced a flint, they were all asked to leave the Great Hall. They left, shouting inflammatory remarks.

And then the interrogation began, this time focusing on facts, trivia and world addenda.

"Who wrote the Book of Love?"

"The Corsairs."

"What is the one language the Bible has not been translated into?"

"Sign language."

"What do England and Spain have in common?"

"The moors."

"What is the medical name for female genitalia?"

"Pudenda."

"And what does that word mean in Latin?'

"It means *shame*."

"What kind of fruit prevailed in the Garden of Eden?"

"Apples."

"What was the secret identity of Zoroaster?"

"Don Diego de la Vega."

"If Pyramus built the pyramids, what did Thisbe build?"

"I don't know that one."

"In what year was Jesus Christ born?"

"In approximately four B.C. Accounts vary. Some put it at eight."

"And what does B.C. mean?"

"Before Christ."

"How can he, then, have been born four to eight years before himself?"

"Time is relative. Timekeepers are worse."

"What is Holland famous for?"

"Elms, Edam cheese, canals, clogs, gingerbread housing, dams, windmills, world-class explorers and religious reformers."

"What was the final score of the Crusades?"

"Six-to-two, Christians."

"What was Ovid's favorite myth?"

"Narcissus."

"How many times is the phrase 'increase and multiply' used in the Old Testament?"

"I don't remember."

"Who invented the yo-yo?"

"Archimedes."

Etc.

Finally, Cortez could endure no more. He came out of the gallery and into the parquet floor of the Great Hall, ripping his shirt as he strode, revealing the welts of the whip that he had used the night before for the first and last time.

"Take me instead," Cortez shouted, "and let this holy man go."

Ignatius of Loyola accepted this outrageous intrusion by a fellow Spaniard as a sign of divine intervention, and he ordered the inquisition officially closed.   Erasmus was reinstated, with full privileges and retroactive benefits. As a sign of good faith, Loyola and Erasmus agreed to hear each other's confessions.   Privately, each thanked Cortez for helping him to save face.

Outside the Great Hall, mobs of Dutch children were singing.

Back in Madrid, Cortez receded once again into relative obscurity, sipping *sol y sombra* with his semi-friend Balboa at the Club de Conquistadores.

"We missed you at the old watering hole," Balboa said.

"Thank you, Bo."

"So, tell, Hernando.   Did you get an answer to your question about the meaning of life?"

"Not exactly, Bo. But I don't seem to need to ask it any longer."

At that moment, a courier came into the club and delivered a letter to Cortez.

He opened it.

Hernando:

Heard about your good work in Holland. You remind me more and more of Odoacer.

Your Secret Admirer

"Bad news?" Balboa asked.

"Not really. A bill came due."

"Oh, that. Everybody has that."

Hernando Cortez was suddenly happy. Happy as . . . happy as . . . a hallelujah of larks. His mind began to wander, as it will in most world-class explorers, until it fixed on the image of two turtledoves, breaking through the domed illusion of a church and soaring up to the vast unanswerable open sky.

✳

Note

What follows is a transcription of the song the Dutch children were singing.

"*Schele, zie jÿ die vliegmachine?*
Schele, zie jÿ er twee misschien?
Schele, ik kan niet velen
dat jÿ er twee ziet en ikke maar één. "

(Crosseyes, do you see that plane?
Crosseyes, do you see two planes maybe?
Crosseyes, I can't stand it
That you see two, and I see only one.)

Acts of Indulgence

She was beside herself, of course. In those days, they didn't have therapists, so she went to the parish priest.

"It's my son," she complained. "I can't stop him from whipping himself."

"Go home, Frau Luther," the priest said. "It's a phase. Surely, it will pass."

Of course, she was concerned about more than the deep welts and scars on her son's body. Young Martin soiled all his bedsheets and stained his best white shirts with all this whipping.

But, you see, boys and girls, he was trying to be holy. He really was.

When Frau Luther got home that day, she asked for her son.

"Martin."

"*Ja, Mutter?*"

"*Was ist das?*"

"*Musik, das ist, Mutter.*"

"You're composing music again?"

"Jawohl."

"What is it called?"

"It's called 'Eine Kleine . . . ' I don't know what else to put in there."

"You don't gesagt. *Und was ist das?*"

"It's a speech, mutter."

"And what is your speech called?"

"It's called '*Ich bin ein berliner*.'"

"You are a dolt full of weltschmerz, but I love you. Come eat some strudel with me."

"Did they really say those things, Mr. Hohenzollern?"

"Ja. Yes, they did. It was long ago, boys and girls, but they really did talk that way. Can you imagine? Young Martin was about your age. What would *your* mothers say if you went around whipping yourselves and writing music and speeches? Bobby?"

"They'd say we were perverts."

"Yes, well, maybe, Bobby. Anyway, next Sunday we'll talk about the Reformation. Yes, Bobby. What is it?"

"When are we gonna talk about sex?"

"When we get to the twentieth century, Bobby. Be patient. We're only about four-hundred years away."

Martin Luther Meets With Sigmund Freud

"My boy, you suffer from delusions of grandeur. A classic case. You were raised with a rather weak ego-formation, and, failing your grand communion with God, you have proclaimed, rather convincingly, to judge the numbers of your followers, that God's grace is not a reward for good works, but a gift to be accepted."

"Yes, but I was only reacting against the entire system of indulgences."

"But you must see, my boy, that your 'gift from God' is, in itself, an indulgence. The only difference is that your indulgence is free."

"I have come to you, good doctor, precisely because I want to be normal, not great. I want to be left alone and saved by God's grace. I don't want a lot of followers."

"That's a lot of wall putty. Have you stopped these whippings?"

"No."

"Have you tried?"

"Yes, but I cannot stop them."

"Tremendous rejection is the root cause of such self-hatred. It stems from your early childhood, I suspect."

"But my mother loved me very much. I must protest . . . "

"Did she feed you mashed potatoes?"

"Yes."

"Whipped potatoes?"

"Yes."

"And did she feed you strawberries in summer, like a good German mummy?"

"Ja, she did."

"And were they smothered in whipped cream?"

"Yes, they always were. She called them 'Santa's beard.'"

"I see. And these adversaries of yours, did you want to whip them?"

"Johann Tetzel. You should have seen him, Herr Freud. A Dominican monk, selling indulgences around Wittenberg, as though he were a street vendor, selling soft pretzels or something."

"Okay, Marty. Express your anger. Complete this sentence. 'Tetzel is a . . . ?'"

"Tetzel is a pretzel."

"There. Good. Very good. And Johann Eck."

"Eck is dreck."

"Danke. You're better than a *bildungsroman,* Marty. Clearly, you have a basic puke reaction against anyone named Johann. Like Strauss?"

"Strauss is a mouse."

"Und Bach?"

"Bach is an old sock."

"And how about, let's see, how about Leo? He excommunicated you."

"The Pope sucks fallibility pills."

"This is tremendous progress, Marty. Are you still hung up on baby baptisms?"

"Yes. They must be allowed into the kingdom."

"And so they shall, my boy. So they shall. Same time next week?"

Martin Luther Meets John F. Kennedy

"Johann, I must tell you plainly. I don't like your name, but I caught your speech in Berlin, and I liked that very much."

"*Ich bin ein berliner?*"

"Ja, that one. I wrote that a long time ago."

"How is it that you're still alive?"

"I had a religious conversion in a thunderstorm."

"Could you be more specific?"

"I got hit by lightning. Instead of killing me, it gave me eternal life. A gift from God. I can time-travel now."

"Like those Vonnegut books?"

"Yes, but I'm not hung up on Dresden. Herr Jung cured me of that."

"So, what are you doing in America?"

"Brecht told me I should come and check out the colonial furniture. Interesting wood, he told me. Especially the mahogany."

"And you thought you'd drop into the Oval Office?"

"Yes, I was really hoping to meet Bobby. He studied me in Sunday school."

"I see. Maybe you'd care to meet my cabinet while you're here."

Martin Luther Meets With Fulton J. Sheen

"You have been influenced by Teilhard de Chardin, Full?"

"Yes, approximately."

"And you like Chesterton?"

"Absurdly so. Especially when he comes out with quips

like, 'Birth control means no birth and no control.'"

"I find you to be kind of an uptight guy."

"I'm sorry you feel that way. Anything in particular?"

"Ja. You look like Ed Sullivan."

Martin Luther Meets With Martin Luther King, Jr.

"Why did you take my name, black man?"

"I have a dream, German soul brother."

"Yes, but you took my whole name."

"I have a dream."

"You keep saying that. But I was just thinking: If the Reformation had not succeeded, I would have been forgotten and Erasmus would have been the great hero of my century. You might have been called Desiderius Erasmus King, Jr."

"Maybe so. Maybe so."

"Are your people in the habit of taking the names of German reformer priests?"

"I'm a reforming sort of minister myself. We both got the struggle in our blood."

"Have you ever been whipped?"

"I don't want to answer that. We're marching out of the past now."

"Are you afraid of lightning?"

"No."

"Good. Then you may continue in my name."

Martin Luther Meets With Jacques Derrida, Dr. Ruth and Yogi Berra

"Have you had time to re-evaluate your dog-ma?"

"You need to meet a nice girl, ja, and don't be naughty, ja, but do be nice, ha ha, in a naughty way, ja?"

"I ain't that kind of yogi, and those are shaving cuts, not whip-welts."

Martin Luther Meets Elisabeth Kübler-Ross

"I am convinced, E., of the following: Just as individual Christians must do their own believing, so, too, must they do their own dying."

"This is fit and proper, right and just, Martin."

"And yet I know so little about dying."

"There are five stages."

"You see, I have apparently survived my death in 1546."

"The final stage is acceptance. You have apparently not accepted."

"What must I do to accept my death?"

"That depends upon your belief system."

"Well, what would you say for my belief system?"

"You must accept your death as a gift from God."

Martin Luther Meets With Werner Herzog

"I want to film your life, Martin."

"You are qualified to do this?"

"I'm the New German skinny. You've seen my flicks."

"Would you turn my life into a surrealist haze?"

"No. I would strive for lucidity. I like that hypnotized look in your eyes. I would convey that."

"Okay, but one thing. You cannot have Bruno S. play the role of Martin Luther."

"Agreed."

"So, who would play me? Kinski?"

"No, he's too blotto. I was thinking more of John Denver."

Martin Luther Meets Sören Kierkegaard

"Sören, you were unfair to Schlegel."

"Yes."

"And you were unfair to Hegel."

"Yessiree, sir."

"And you were unfair to Kant."

"Na, nana, booboo."

"And you were unfair to Lacan."

"*Lacan est sur la table.*"

"Were you fair to anyone?"

"*La tasse est sur la Saussure.*"

"That's what I thought. Sören, I want to tell you plainly. I have hungered and thirsted for a personal God."

"The great ones are asked to go a little more hungry and thirsty than the rest. It's a Zen joke. God is partial to Zen humor. The eleventh hour parable, you dig? So, here's the Zen joke. The greatest gifts go to the least deserving people."

"That's not fair."

"I know. That's why I've been unfair to everyone."

Martin Luther Meets With John Calvin

"Johann, I must tell you. I don't like your first name."

"Well, I'm not crazy about your last name, Martin."

"Why is it we never met in life, J.C.?"

"Reformers aren't allowed to mingle. Too much solidarity makes for too much conformity."

"Do you have any regrets?"

"Yeah. I wanted to live in the twentieth century. I could have had a Walkman. I could have been a TV evangelist. I could have eaten meat on Friday."

"Cal, I have hungered and thirsted for a personal God."

"That again?"

Martin Luther Meets Mother Teresa

"Mother Teresa, I have hungered and thirsted for a personal God."

"It shows. The pasty look. The withered skin. I'd say you've been dead for about four-hundred years."

"That's just it. I'm not totally dead. My truth goes

marching on. I was evicted from a Ramada Inn the other day, for whipping myself."

"I see. You know, Martin, people don't do that anymore. Whipping oneself no longer has religious connotations. It has sexual connotations now."

"Tell me something, Mama T. You're a living legend. I don't think there's a living soul who would bet against your sainthood. So, what is it with me? Do you think God is Catholic?"

"It's a distinct possibility, my boy."

"Do you think he holds the Reformation against me?"

"All this time? I doubt even God could keep a grudge that long."

"I believe you. I even feel my soul is purified. So, what is left to do? I'm getting confused by all these interviews and opinions. We didn't have so many when I was alive and in time with my century. Heck, what got me excommunicated, the very same things make Pope Johann, I hate that name, the Twenty-third a radical hero. Why was I damned, when he gets blessed for doing exactly what I proposed?"

"Timing. It's all a question of timing. Yours was bad, his was good."

"Alas and woe. What advice can you give me?"

"Win the love of a wonderful woman. God has a soft spot for lovers."

"But that would involve an . . . intermingling of the flesh."

"I suppose it would."

"Are you suggesting necrophilia and petulance?"

"We call it necking and petting."

"Are you suggesting concupiscence?"

"Whatever slays you."

Martin Luther Meets Ava G.

"Hello. Who are you?"

"I'm Ava G."

"I'm Martin Luther. How are you? Do you want to be saved?"

"I'm fine, and aren't you a little old to be standing on street corners and hitting on women with a line like that?"

"Okay, then. What is your favorite Christmas carol?"

"'Silent Night,' I guess."

"I wrote it. Would you like to see my organ?"

"I ought to mace you, but there's a kind of pathetic urgency in your Teutonic appeal, a kind of hypnotic bliss in your eyes, a quiet desperation in your manhood. These things appeal to women."

"They do? Ava, I must tell you plainly. I have hungered and thirsted for a personal g . . . irl like you."

"I bet you have."

"Would you instruct me in the ways of love?"

"You're not an alien, are you?"

"Why do you say that?"

"You talk like some of those trolls on TV."

"No, I come from Germany."

"Well, that's nice. Let's have coffee first. We'll see about the ways of love after that. I'll say one thing for you, Martin. You're different from the guys I've been meeting."

"Danke, Ava. Thank you very much."

"What are those welts on your face? Cat scratch you?"

"No, uh, those are shaving cuts."

"Where did you get that Brooklyn accent, Martin?"

"I learned it from a yogi I met."

"Good line, Martin. I'm beginning to like you."

"Gesundheit. So, this is acceptance . . . "

The Pleasures of Anonymity

In his last years, Hernando Cortez, disavowed by his own government and disenchanted with world travel, met Miguel Thirteen-Middle Names Cervantes at a conference on *modernismo* in Salamanca. Cervantes was sipping a Shirley Temple with two straws. It was this duality of drawn straws that attracted Cortez to the bespectacled Cervantes.

"Hernando Cortez, world traveler," Cortez said, extending his hand.

"Miguel de Unamuno del Campo Abierto y Mucho Más Cervantes, would-be novelist."

"How come so many middle names?"

"Tradition. And many remarriages."

"I see. *Yo veo.* Well," Cortez said, sitting down and sipping his own straight Juanillo Daniels, "you have a studied earnestness about you, Mike."

"Jes," Cervantes said, managing his English very badly, "it is a nervous tic. Did you know, Hernando, that fame and famine are the same word?"

"*¿La fama?*"

"*Claro que sí. La pura fama. Lo mismo. Igual.*"

"You have, may I say, an editorial redundance about you as well."

"And you have keen powers of observation."

"It comes from all my world travels," Cortez said.

"I have never been to Portugal," Cervantes confessed.

"Really?"

"Nor to Barcelona."

"My God."

"Nor to Toledo, even."

Cortez didn't know what to say. Cervantes had an interesting aristocratic air about him, but it was perhaps due to an insular personality. Cortez stared at Cervantes. Yes. The writer *did* have a rather convoluted homebody look.

"*¿Quién es su autor preferido?*" Cervantes said suddenly, abruptly shifting the conversation to talk shop.

"I don't have a ready name for you," Cortez said.

"Take your time."

"Nope," Cortez said finally, scratching his chin, "nobody comes to mind."

"*Quelle lacune,*" Cervantes said, obviously better at French than English.

"I got it," Cortez said, his eyes energized.

"Great. Good. Who?"

"Anónimo."

"Who? That's not a name."

"Of course it is. *¿Romance anónimo? La Perfidia de Porfirio, por anónimo. Al pasar la noche en muchas ciudades muy lejas, por anónimo.* That one."

"My dear Hernando," Cervantes said, affecting *la voz preciosa,* "you cannot say Anonymous is your favorite author. This is simply not done."

The Italian waitress came to ask if they wanted refills before Cortez could answer Cervantes.

"*Niente,*" Cortez said to her, covering his glass with a flat hand.

"*Me gustan los anónimos, mon cher,*" he said to Cervantes.

"*Soit,*" Cervantes said. "*Punto,*" he added. "And what, may I ask, is your favorite genre?"

"I'm partial to maritime graffiti," Cortez said. "Poems against the king, carved after setting sail."

"I see. And what, among the more conventional forms, strikes your fancy?"

"*Pelo pomes*. The 'skinnies,' you know? And maybe a few sobriquets. And, here and there, a *romance gitano*."

"I am writing a novel," Cervantes said proudly.

"A novel? Something new? Isn't everything written novel?"

"No, my friend. It is to be a new form. More prose than poetry. Real dialogue. A longer work, with sections called chapters. Some intense observation, some picaresque, some tragic flaws, a few guffaws."

"Sounds like vaudeville to me. They had that in Mexico. They told stories for days on end, some of them Aztecs. Like that?"

"I was thinking more of the instructional value than the entertainment value. I prefer to think of my novel as 'exemplar.' I like that word: 'exemplar.'"

"It's a nice word, but I'm not sure it will bring you the *fama* you seem to be seeking."

"Have you, then, never heard of Guillermo Shakespeare?"

"Is he an explorer?"

"Of forms, yes. He is an English litterist."

"No, I have, then, never heard of him."

"He writes plays. Of course, he writes sonnets as well. But he is versatile enough to write plays, too. Me, I'm horrible at plays. I put one on once for the disabled children in my neighborhood, and they all walked out. It was an emotional experience of the worst sort. So, I am inventing this form called the novel. My book will initiate the era of big books."

"Veritable tomes?"

"Yes."

"Like the Good Book?"

"Maybe longer."

"*The Longest Story Ever Told?*"

"Something like that. But not just length. Width and epigrammatic depth as well."

"What's your novel called?"

"At the moment, it has the working title of *La Vida es Sueño.*"

"That's a problem, as I see it."

"How so, Hernando?"

"Too suggestive of other things the reader might be doing. You might as well say, *La Vida es Sexo*, and capitalize on the pelo market."

"That's a little too commercially conscious, for my tastes."

"Who's the main character?"

"A young poet and dreamer. Don Quixote."

"Why not call it simply, *Don Quixote?*"

"And give away my character's name?"

"I don't see why not. Any book with 'Life' in the title is a bit too broadsweep, don't you think, Mike?"

"Oh, I don't know about that."

"Did that Greek guy, what's his name, Omar? Did he put 'life' in the title of *Illiad* or *Odyssey?*"

"No. No, he didn't."

"Well then?"

"But his full name is Don Quixote de la Mancha."

"Don't tell me he has as many family names as you do."

"No, that's it. De la Mancha."

"Sleeve? Not very catchy, Mike, unless you're being ironic and maybe a bit self-reflective about the jacket to the book."

"I never should have told you. Every time I talk about my book, it gets confusing. I should just say, a work in progress."

"Is that what other writers say?"

Cervantes nodded his head. He looked very convoluted.

"What's your novel about?"

"Windmills."

Cortez didn't say anything. Instead, he looked around for the Italian waitress.

"You don't like it?" Cervantes asked.

"A little airy-fairy, is all."

"It's supposed to be a symbol. For poetry and dreaming. The unattainable. The ineffable."

"Like the little red wheelbarrow of *modernismo*?"

"You are remarkably literate," Cervantes said, "for someone who never reads."

"Life has taught me many things."

"Would you like to be my mentor, Nando?"

"Shucks, yes. I've got nothing better to do."

✸

"You need a love interest, Mike," Cortez said, putting down several chapters of *Quixote*. "Reading about two men, riding around on horses like that, is too dry. I don't know any world-class explorers who would read this stuff. Maybe in a spritely *romance gitano*, but not in this thing you call a novel. By the way, I'm not sure you can turn the adjective into a noun. Can you get away with calling it *A* novel?"

"There are risks in every innovation," Cervantes reminded him.

"Well, you still need some love scenes. Think of a woman."

"Okay. I am thinking of a woman . . . "

Cortez waited a long time.

"Well?"

"I am thinking of a woman . . . "

"Who is she?" Cortez said, almost screaming.

"I thought you were going to guess. I have a woman in mind. She is very sweet."

"Dulce. That's good. Very provocative."

"It's no good. Already been used, I think."

"Well, we are most certainly not going to worry about a trivial detail like that."

Cortez came out of the old school. Imitation was okay by him. Only Cervantes worried about originality. Cortez argued that anything that original was bound to be imitated anyway, so why the posh bother? Well, because it was a novel, Cervantes countered, and, by definition, anything in a novel ought to be original. Well, okay, Cortez conceded.

They settled on Dulcinea. Don Quixote would be in love with Dulcinea.

"I think, too, that you have to give Panza a reason for being there."

Cervantes was puzzled.

"I thought I did. He, too, is a poet and a dreamer."

"No, I think one of them ought to be a poet and a dreamer, while the other one could be earthbound, heavy, stuck in his senses, raucous, even a little dim-witted."

"Epicurean?" Cervantes asked.

"Whatever," Cortez said. He didn't like to stall on characters. He was more concerned with plotting.

So, Sancho Panza became a lusty old salt, lively as a samba, lucid as a brick.

The novel was progressing nicely.

❋

Sometimes, the circumstances of a friendship are stranger than the people in the friendship. And yet neither Cortez nor Cervantes ever questioned the efficacy of their bond. From Cortez, Cervantes wanted truth-telling and worldly experience. And Cortez looked to Cervantes for the naïveté of youth, the passion of art, the other worldly dreams of his characters. Playing critic was a small price to pay for the sometimes delirious, always fevered rendering of those dreams in their first rough-cut versions. Once in a while, Cortez would talk about slaughtering Aztecs or about the betrayal of kings or about the primitive pleasures of native women in various ports of call. Or Cervantes would talk about solitude, about his boyhood dreams of being a Jesuit, about the Inquisition or God's feigned intentions for Spain in the long march of history. Sometimes, they both talked about coffee.

But, more than anything else, this would-be novel, the first of its kind, was the bond between them.

Cortez was feeling especially sentimental one day. It was his birthday. He felt that melancholy of knowing how many lay behind him, how few ahead.

"It must give you tremendous satisfaction," he said to Cervantes, "knowing that you're doing your life's work."

"I can't talk to you right now, Nando," Cervantes answered. "I'm writing."

And it went like that between them. When Cortez felt old and sentimental, Cervantes barely heard him. And, when Cervantes was between images and feeling especially vulnerable, Cortez played the critic and was harsh on him.

"I think," he said, holding the hand-written pages of two chapters in his hands, "that these will not do."

"Oh God," Cervantes said, all hopes dashed. "Why this time?"

"Because, Mike, you are too earnest. Too obvious. You must perchance find a way to be more ironic. More than that, you must learn to couch yourself, to leave a little symbolism for posterity."

"I am running out of ink," Cervantes complained.

"I will get you some."

"And my quill leaks," Cervantes pouted.

"I'll get you a new one."

"And what if I gave up the whole enterprise?"

"I think I might kill you. With my bare hands."

"You are too old for that."

"Then you must write me into your novel. The old man, searching for the fountain of youth."

"How trite," Cervantes said.

He could be incredibly cruel sometimes.

✳

One day they went to the corrida. There were four bulls that afternoon, resulting in three cut ears and one gored matador.

Cortez leaned over to Cervantes.

"In Mexico the matadors sometimes ride horses," he said.

"Poor bulls," Cervantes said.

"Why?"

"It's difficult to gore a horse."

Cortez sat back and thought about Cervantes' response. Sometimes, the milk of human kindness went a little skimmed and sour in the young writer with thirteen middle names.

"Can you imagine your man of La Mancha as a matador?"

"Yes. He would try anything for the love of dear Dulcinea."

"Even submit to being gored?"

"Even that," Cervantes said, without batting an eyelash.

Cortez had never realized how deeply the romanticism ran in his friend, just underneath the thin veneer of *modernismo*.

✳

"I am going on a trip," Cortez announced one day. "A friend in the trade will give me free passage. I will be back in a month or two."

"Must you? I have just begun to layer my narrative. Daily it becomes more ironic. But I am no judge of affect. Who will tell me if it is good or not?"

"Go to the docks," Cortez said. "Read to the sailors on the biggest ships, the ones that are going around the world and may never come back. They will tell you. Then read to the women left behind. They will also tell you."

"I am not ready to give public readings," Cervantes said, petulantly.

"Suit yourself."

Cervantes became morose. He hadn't realized just how much he depended upon Cortez, not just for criticism, but also for companionship. Always a believer in Don Quixote, he began to emulate Sancho Panza in the absence of Hernando. He ate epicurean meals, at all hours and in immoderate quantities. He went to prostitutes and read his fiction for as long as they could stand him. He befriended Moors and other derelicts in the streets. He wrote passionate poems to Cortez and tore them up. He took absinthe for the first time in his life. When Cortez came back, it was with new scrolls of parchment, several bottles of India ink, the most elaborate quills.

"I have been to England, my friend. Let me tell you about this Shakespeare. He is *anónimo*. I saw ten plays by him and I never saw him. Doesn't that seem odd to you? Someone who writes plays, but never attends them? I found scores of serious apprentices, all writing plays, all signing them 'Will S. Bard of Avon.' And I chanced upon a madman named Marlowe, who swears he wrote all the plays. And then the plays, themselves, Mike. There was one about Venice. I tell you plainly, whoever wrote that play never bothered to go to Venice. The details were all historically false, geographically inaccurate. He's even written one about a Moor, for God's sake. I told these people my man would soon be writing something about William of Orange. That put them ill at ease, straightaway. Don't worry, I never said a word about novels."

"Dear God, Nando, you did this for me?"

"Not entirely. I heard a rumor at the docks that the blackguard Henry Hudson, a veritable bastard explorer, if ever there was one, had been commissioned by the queen to put Shakespeare back on track about the facts of faraway places. Apparently, this queen is a mick for details and doesn't want the rest of the world thinking that the English are complete ninnies when it comes to geography."

"Was the rumor true?"

"Only partially. The part about the queen is true. But Henry Hudson is on holiday in Holland. They've got some second-rate navigator named Griffin Bell in residence at Stratford. The point is, your place in history is safe, Mike. Shakespeare is *anónimo*."

"I am truly touched, Nando. No greater love hath . . . "

"Don't crap out on me, Mike."

✳

They rode by coach to Barcelona. Maritime lessons, Cortez said. A simply must-see place. He said he was nostalgic for seagulls and kelp. Pirates roamed the port with patches over one eye, both real and imagined.

"Hey old man," some sailors called out to him, "you don't know *súbito* from *sotto voce*."

"Never mind these tars," Cortez said to Cervantes. "They're quite provincial. The best ones are always at sea. The worst sit around playing pinochle, waiting for a crew to be put together."

Cervantes found the whole scene quite pathetic.

✳

One day, when Cortez had read an especially thoughtful section on Dulcinea, he decided that she was as ineffable as the windmills. Cervantes couldn't speak to it. He said he felt too close to the material to judge. They talked at length, and they decided they needed a woman's opinion. Cortez said he knew a woman. Her name was Magdalena Opharim, and she was a Sephardic sorceress.

"I do better reading palms," she said, but they insisted that she read the section.

"Well?" Cortez said, when she proved reticent to speak.

"She is too much of a shiksa."

Cervantes demanded a second opinion, so they went to see Felicia, Cortez's younger sister. She lived in a big hacienda near El Escorial, where she dabbled with passenger pigeons, sending notes of undying love to one of the monks at the monastery nearby.

She read the section.

"I like Quixote," she said. "I think he's a priest, secretly posing as a poet and dreamer."

"But what about Dulcinea?" Cervantes asked.

"She's too vapid," Felicia said.

When they were back in Madrid, Cortez tried to console Cervantes.

"Not every character can be unforgettably winning. If she is vapid, it is only because Quixote and Panza are so fully realized. Infer from that."

Cervantes sank into a deep depression instead.

❋

Then, without any apparent reason, Cervantes decided to put narratives within the narrative. He already had, of course, a novel about a poet living his dreams and reciting the most incredible *romance gitano* lines, but now he envisioned a novel about a novelist writing a novel, even though the novel had not yet been invented.

"This is a rather masturbatory idea," Cortez cautioned him.

"Why? It simply makes things more interior, that's all."

"You are so far removed from the world already."

"But the novel is best suited for such meditations. One day, novelists will write novels about the writing of novels, and I shan't be remembered as the first to do it."

"It is a sign of decadence," Cortez said. "You don't need to be remembered for it."

✳

Cortez suffered from insomnia, arthritis and gout, but insomnia was by far the worst. He was tormented in dreams, unsteady in his interpretation of dreams, and heartily contrite for having slaughtered so many Aztecs in his younger years.

"Their souls walk with me in sleep," he told Cervantes. "Each night I ask forgiveness, and each night I must accompany one of them across the great river, hand in hand, walking on top of water. But I cannot swim, and I am deathly afraid of drowning. Each time I think the Aztec will have his revenge on me by letting go of my hand and watching me drown."

"But it never happens?" Cervantes asked.

"No. They need to get to the other side. Forgiving me is part of the price they have to pay, in order to inhabit the spirit world fully. One Aztec told me in a dream that he, too, feared letting go of my hand, and, in watching me drown, he would never get to the other side."

"Then passage is safe?"

"Yes, but there are so many of them to cross. At one per night, my nights are full. You can imagine. Sometimes, I try to talk whole families into crossing. But this is not permitted. I fear that I shall run out of nights, before I have crossed all of them."

"*No te preocupes, Nando.* If you do, I shall carry them for you."

"You would do that for me?"

"Yes. I have no life experience of my own. I should gladly take on yours."

"You are an imbecile and a saint, Mike, and I treasure you both."

✳

Just when Cortez began to have intimations of mortality, seeing his death in every passing coach, Cervantes stalled on the novel and began massive revisions of previous chapters.

"You don't have time to go backwards now," Cortez told him.

"But I must. That is the lesson of history. I cannot go forth, until I have fully gone backwards."

"This is poppycock of the most mendacious sort."

Cortez began to fear that he would die before Cervantes had finished *Don Quixote*. So, he made up a story to tell his friend.

"I didn't want to tell you this, Mike. But now I feel I must. There is another writer in the realm, and he is writing his *Quixote*, the very same book, with the same characters, the same dialogue, everything. He is completely attuned to your mind, and he creates by copying your thoughts. I fear that he will finish his *Quixote* before you have finished yours, and then you will be thrown into prison as a plagiarist."

"This cannot be. How can this be?"

"It simply is. I had evidence of this sort of thing in my explorer days. So many of us set forth for the Indies. We all landed in separate places, and we all claimed to have discovered America. And you might say, 'How can this be?' But it was. And the worst was Balboa, the complete baobab, if you ask me. His little botched isthmus was hardly what any of us would call discovering a continent. In his case, things got out of hand. He claimed discovery of the Pacific Ocean, even as a Chinaman was crossing from the other side, and claiming discovery of the Atlantic. You must finish your novel first."

"*Soit*," Cervantes said. "But who is this dungbag who dares to write my novel?"

"His name is Pierre Menard, and he feels the same way toward you."

"Maybe we ought to kill him."

"Finish your novel. That will kill him."

Cervantes began creating as he had never created before.

Fourteen hours a day he wrote. And wrote and wrote some more. Cortez was ecstatic. He felt no shame for having lied to his friend. A lie in the service of a first novel is no lie at all, but a muse by another voice.

✳

When the novel came out, at great risk and considerable expense to the publisher, it was an immediate success, both as an individual work and as a form.

The signing party was in Salamanca, and Cervantes was suddenly surrounded by foreign journalists and Jesuits. None of them seemed to take any notice of Cortez, so intent were they on getting quotes from Cervantes.

"Is there anyone in particular," an Italian journalist asked him, "to whom you would like to dedicate your exemplary work?"

"To Pierre Menard," Cervantes said.

Cortez whispered into his friend's ear.

"I made him up, to force you to finish your book. He doesn't exist."

Cervantes looked at him. They had never exchanged a more meaningful look.

"For that matter," Cortez shrugged, "neither do I."

Cervantes excused himself from the journalists and walked with Cortez into the bar.

"What do you mean, you don't exist?"

"I'm an apparition, Mike, particular to you. I died the year you were born. Only I had all those Aztec crossings in the way, so they said I'd have to go round one more time and get a good deed done. So, you finished our book. That's the good deed. Now I can shake this apparition phase and just finish up when you do."

It was true. He was already beginning to disappear. He was perforated lines, floating hyphens, dust specks.

"I'm going to miss you," Cervantes said, with tears in his eyes.

"Impossible," Cortez said. "I swim in your soul."

"Well, at least we beat Shakespeare, didn't we?"

"I hate to tell you this, kid," Cortez said, more voice than body now, "but the period will be remembered as the Elizabethan Age. You see, the worst claptrap in English has a wider readership than the best work in Spanish. But don't despair. You still got the patent on the novel. Nobody can take that away from you."

When he was completely done, Cervantes felt as though he had just digested a full meal, and he smiled from ear to ear. He was thinking about the various authors of *Lazarillo*, whose names would remain anonymous. He was thinking about the last Aztec to cross. And he was thinking about Henry Hudson, drunk under some windmill in Holland. Then Hudson disappeared, and the windmill remained.

✳

Hernando Cortez Cortez (1485–1547)
Miguel Saavedra de Cervantes (1547–1616)
William Shakespeare (1564–1616)

The Discovery of Chocolate

$\mathcal{W}$e had been hunting wild boar and wildebeest in the mountains west of Muskies when the headhunters fell on us like a coconut storm in the tropics and lay into us with pygmy arrows and poisoned darts. It was the kind of attack one might have expected in the wet dense overgrowth of the Amazon jungles, but it was the last thing we expected in the rust-arid cliffs of the Sierras in Northern Mexico. Even Cortez, a career conquistador, expressed amazement and took to crossing himself, like the tic of a lunatic.

They killed our scouts, our sentries and slaves, one by one, in the most furtive manner. They attacked us while we slept or bathed, while we were in the act of voiding ourselves, and, even, upon rare occasions, in the act of sexual intercourse. They had an uncanny patience for this sort of stalking and random selection, waiting for just those moments when we would be most predisposed. Sometimes, while we were hiking ourselves up hills of pine straw and brown chalk, we could hear a straining, a grinding, a moaning, and we knew these were the sounds of their stomachs growling. But we never saw them. We could only guess at their stunted shadows, forming a prong with our own. We saw the occasional wildebeest, a grouse or armadillo, and, of course, the constant circling birds of prey overhead, but we never saw hide nor hair of the squat heathens who dared to eat Catholics.

One night I chanced to share my blanket with a Jesuit priest named Calzado. He was dank with fever, and he mused about the naming of mountains, finding it peculiar that we Spaniards always seemed to name our Sierras Madre or Nevada, Madre or Nevada. And then, as though he had stumbled onto a metaphysical discovery, he asked with wide eyes what my name was.

"Quemada," I told him.

"The one who burns," he translated. "So you see . . . "

What my name had to do with Madre or Nevada as the namesakes for mountains, I didn't see.

The next morning, the body of Calzado still shared the blanket with me, but it was headless. The headhunters had come in the night, hacked off his head and left me to sleep. More than sorry for the priest, I felt siamese with his twitching torso and sanctified for it.

"Corta-cabezas," Cortez said, looking at my blanket and coining the phrase by which the headhunters would henceforth be known.

We carried the banner of Montezuma with us, and we assumed that any living soul in Mexico would pay it allegiance, but we were wrong. I don't think the *corta-cabezas* knew a thing about Montezuma and the Aztec Empire. They knew wild boar and wildebeest, and they knew to decapitate Catholics.

Cortez ordered me to bum the blanket, with the body of Calzado still wrapped inside. I doubt that Cortez was even thinking of my family name when he gave this order, but setting fire to the priest made me think about his last words, and, of course, I did see clearly then: I put the torch to Calzado and felt free for it, wild and somehow more heathen than the heathens for the fire that was my namesake.

"Madre-Nevada," I screamed, as the flames ran around the blanket like a plague of locusts in a wheat field, and what I said was itself coined into our language as the cure-all anathema to *corta-cabezas*.' Even, Cortez, himself, was heard intoning those words several times, repeatedly, as he voided himself on the stubby cliffs.

"Madre-Nevada, madre-nevada, madre-nevada."

"The mother who snows," I translated to myself. The son who burns, the mother who snows, and who knows what good it did? We had no trouble from the headhunters after that.

Cortez was never one to run from danger. The risk gave him pulse, threw him back against his wits, brought out his best. When he saw that the headhunters had bagged more of us than we had bagged wild boar, he called the expedition to a quit. As we came down from the mountains, he assembled us and, stroking his beard philosophically, he said that he had learned a great deal about hunting from the *corta-cabezas.* Then he baptized their souls *in absentia,* and we left the region altogether.

＊

Me? I am called Jaime Posado, don't you know? I killed Moors for a living before I hired on as a swabber with Cortez. Barcelona to Cádiz and back, I went with the pay armies for Christ, exterminating Moors. It was a good living.

One time, I come back from three months of fierce fighting to my little pueblo in the hills, only to find my wife in bed with a blind man, who was vagabonding his way cross-country, living off widows and liberals and such. There I was, full of killing anyway, lots of *mano a mano* with Moors, and welts to prove it, and I find my wife cuddle-straddle to this *desgraciado.*

I killed her first. Crushed her face flatter than a mesa with the wedge-end of a *molinillo.* Then I shanked her out of bed and took her place. You know, just like in all the fairy tales. The blind man heard the thump, and he was asking more *quepasas* than an auctioneer, all the while feeling for me with his finger. Hot milk, but I never seen such frantic fingers before. Maybe they's what Graciela saw in him. Anyway, he feels the hair on my chest and jerks back, like he touched fire or something.

By the time he climbed his way up my face with those spidery fingers of his, he was going more sour than a lemon with sweat. And, before he could say *ayjodido,* I excavated his eyeholes with the shoot-end of my slingshot, and he was wearing my wood just as pretty as a pair of glasses as he bled to death.

These are murdering times, don't you know? Even so, I was looking at a rope, noose-eye view and dangling, when I opted for this excursion to the New World. I lied about sailing experience, and I thought Cortez was going to saw me in half with his eyes, but when he asked me if I had any familiarity with weapons and I told him I was more aunts and uncles than most men, he believed me. He said he was looking for a few good men who combined the morals of a missionary with the courage of a criminal, and I guess he figured a surplus of the one would make up for a shortfall in the other.

Weren't no boy's choir he assembled. Turned out a good half of his crew was killers and thieves, some of them a lot more gamey than me.

Sailing was the hard part. Not the swabbing so much as the seasickness and the lack of land, that God-forsaken lonely lack of land. When we put into Havana harbor, Cortez proclaimed that we had discovered the New World, the honest Indies he called it, and we pitched the flag of Spain, even though there were already plenty of people in Cuba, and a few flags as well.

When we pushed off again, we put heavy hearts to the wheel. We hadn't gotten rich off looting and pillaging, we were full of scurvy and fever, and most of us still didn't know box from topknot. Cortez, though, he knew how to play the fool much as act the tyrant. Up and down the deck he went, fingers flopping on his mouth organ, harmonicating us with old tar tunes, making us forget that we was sailing the long way home.

We didn't know Mexico was over here, but he knew. Ingots of gold, he'd say, you'll be building your houses with ingots of gold. Hell, we didn't even stop to think if a house made of gold bars would be weatherized or not. We just swabbed and felt greedy, each day more greedy. We were fine-tuned for killing Aztecs when we landed.

We had a chronic bed wetter on board named Curcio, and, rather than shoot the bastard, Cortez claimed him and told him stories of dry deserts in the Sahara. Curcio got so much dryness pumped into him that he forgot to go at night.

And one day, Cortez singled me out for all the other men to see. He lay his hand on my shoulder, all those arm bracelets rattling on my shoulder, and he told the crew that I was the cross-section of the Spanish race. He said that. He looked me in the eye and said that, in all the generations of Iberia past and present and to come, I was as good a common denominator as he would ever find, and the men would do well to stand in behind my example. I never forgot that.

Two days after we'd landed, I took me an Aztec wife. She was neither cultured nor ambitious, but that was fine by me. The Aztecs are a body-simple people. They don't elevate the necessities out of proportion. She knew what sex was, she'd been doing it since she was eight, and at twenty she was pretty practiced for a new bride. I didn't figure I'd have to worry about finding any blind men in my bed. Cortez was so pleased he agreed to stand best man.

✳

My name is Gabriel Trucha, but my nickname is Tiburon. I have been a wrestler all my life. Once I broke three men's backs in a single bear-hug. I had beaten the best wrestlers in Europe when I decided that I wanted to be champion of any New World as well.

It wasn't easy. Cortez didn't look kindly upon my five-hundred pounds. He thought I might sink his ship if I ever fell out of my bunk at night. I had to sign a paper, promising that I would be the first to go overboard, and without a lifeboat at that, if the ship ever swayed or listed to the point of peril. I can't swim, so it was difficult to make such a promise, but I figured, if push ever came to shove, he and a hundred other men would have a hard time making me keep that promise.

Cortez gave me a dispensation from his mountain-climbing expedition in Muskies, so that I could stay in the capital and train for the Games.

We didn't just come to watch the Games. We came to participate in the Aztec Olympics and win their medals from them. Montezuma protested that we didn't meet the eligibility requirements, but Cortez overrode him. We would be allowed to enter the various sports, play by the Aztec rules, and keep the medals we won. Cortez was mostly interested in melting down those gold medals, but I was there for pride.

The Aztecs had never heard of Greco-Roman wrestling, so their rules were a little strange. First off, the weights of the wrestlers had to be equal to the millikilo. But the Aztecs didn't have anybody who weighed five-hundred pounds. So, they countered with three men who weighed one-fifty each and a boy of eight who weighed fifty. Then, too, kicking, scratching and biting are allowed in Aztec wrestling, things that are forbidden in European wrestling. And they don't go to the mat for a mandatory three-count win. Instead, they try to break a limb. A broken arm or leg, paralysis of the spine, castration through biting, nipples sucked off or loose eyeballs, these are all signs of victory in Aztec wrestling. In fact, the crowning "blow" in their system is when you salivate upon your opponent's face, and, while he is still half-conscious, you kiss him on the forehead.

Aztec wrestling, then, had less to do with brute strength than with one's appetite for cruelty, given or received, both perceived and real. The Aztecs are by and large a passive peaceful people, and they have to will themselves into a warrior state through drugs and dreams. Drugs are allowed. Dreams are encouraged.

I had never seen this use of trance-adrenalin in Europe. I admired the way Aztec men who were half-lame with arthritis could suddenly high-kick their opponents' ears. This causing the opponent to "hear the music from within" was much respected among the Aztec athletes. I got a little tranced myself, just watching the featherweights going after each other like two roosters in a cockfight, hopping up and down, ruffling and posturing, then doing flying scissors kicks at each other's throat like two wishbones on a collision course. The dead feather never knew what hit him. The winner had his legs still wrapped around the dead man's throat, waving to the crowds, while the dead man's tongue stuck out from the strangulation, as though in mock protest of the proceedings.

And then, pray Jesus on his mother's milk, I saw something I had never seen in Europe. The winner at an Aztec sporting event gets the spectator's clothes. The winning featherweight pointed at a young girl of twelve, and she stripped down to the skin in front of a hundred-thousand people. The winning feather walks off, waving her robes and petticoats like a cowboy waves rope at a rodeo.

When it was my turn to wrestle, I watched the eight-year old boy take peyote and steroids, blissing himself into some kind of robotic hum for our bout. I decided to discourage the grown-ups by gouging this boy's eyes out. But they seemed to gain new courage at this crass display of brawn. Suddenly, I was looking at flying scissors kicks in triplicate. Luckily, my neck girth was too much for their puny legs, and they found themselves dangling upside-down from my throat. I broke one's back over my knee and sent another into coma with a full-nelson. But the last Aztec spit garlic mist in my eyes, and, while I was temporarily blinded, he tried to castrate me with his teeth. I had that little clam snapping at my groin repeatedly. In desperation I looked up to the esplanade where royalty sat, and I saw the daughter of Montezuma, her mouth wide open in a silent scream.

I couldn't tell if she was afraid I might lose my *cojones* or if she was afraid I might win and demand her clothes. She put her hands to her ears, as if to shut out the roar of the crowd, and I took my lead from her, I slapped that Aztec so hard on both ears that he lost his equilibrium. He buckled back, his bell still ringing, and I broke his legs, to the delight of the crowd.

When I looked up and pointed to Montezuma's daughter, she had already unbuttoned her robes. She was half-tranced and stepping in dreams. The carnal look she gave me, I had never seen on a human being before. Only on bulls and birds of prey. A kind of cool butcher's look.

Again Montezuma protested. Once again Cortez overrode him. I had won the gold we usually stole and I had stripped Montezuma's daughter of her clothes in front of all his subjects, but I had played by the rules and won fairly. For once, the crowd upheld Cortez and went against their emperor.

Cortez gave me my weight in gold as a wedding present. He said I had become a god that day in the arena. He talked a lot about the lions and Christians, and he said I had tied a knot in history. He was crazier than I thought.

*

When I told Cortez that I was no good at killing Aztecs, he agreed. He nodded and said that the pen was mightier than the sword.

"Gaspar de Carvelho," he pronounced, "henceforth you shall keep the records. You shall be the official historian of his expedition."

Quemada looked so jealous that I thought he was going to set me on fire the first chance he got.

I kept track of every single ingot of gold we stole and every Aztec we slaughtered. I described with diligence the constitution of our meals. I kept a record of each correspondence with the King and Queen, each pistol fired, every bowl of beans and rice pudding we ingested. In the beginning I focused on Cortez and followed him wherever he went. But later, as I began to realize what full history entailed, I started interviewing some of the men, noticing what Montezuma was doing apart from Cortez, explicating Aztec customs and rituals. At one time I was, I think, both the most visible man in Mexico and the most reclusive.

The more I wrote, the more I mused on writing, itself. What is the purpose, for example, of a written history? If it was record keeping for later accountability with the King, as I first thought, then I had only to list excursions, surveys, robbings, killings, and shipping to and fro, recipe fashion, without regard to prose. These early columnar jottings seemed to me in retrospect as naïve and primitive, not unlike the pre-history of writing, itself. If the purpose of my history was to give Cortez proof of having been in Mexico, a gift unique to Cortez alone, then the imperative changed, and I needed to reproduce memories, aggrandize achievements, exalt the mundane and omit certain things. At the same time that I discovered the selectivity of history, the minutiae of certain moments and the random gaps in others, I also realized the quotidian nature of all existence: more specifically, that one could be bored, even in the New World.

I wondered thus: On days when nothing happens, should I describe mood? Should I speculate about what might happen? Or shall I recount a detail in more detail? For example, during Easter week, the Spanish are lethargic. They suffer from Lenten withdrawal, as though cocoon-spun and gossamer, about to molt. Yet there are certain grumblings, certain perceivable tendencies . . .

I am sure that Quemada wants to burn me. It is not just because I am official historian, which seems to restrict his behavior when I am around. It is also because I am a Jesuit priest, and I remind him of Calzado, with whom he slept and then torched. Quemada has the ardor of the zealot in his eyes. I am positive that he wants to turn me into toast.

Apart from the certainties, I also have suspicions. For example, Jaime Posado has emerged as the disgruntled voice for the most ignorant of the crew. He is fond of saying that he speaks for the masses, and the masses begin to seem rebellious. Shall I include his suspicion in my history? What if it turns out to be true and Cortez was not aware of it? Will this not, then, be an indictment of Cortez, whose job it is to know all things?

And what about the other remaining Jesuits on this expedition? Do I not have a spiritual obligation to them? Could my history be a history for them? Might I not include some quotes from the Scriptures and daily homilies?

I worry most about Punto, who has become a charismatic in this pagan land and has renamed himself Padre Punt and who walks around in bikini shorts, sneaking holy water into the Aztecs' tequila supply. I tried to talk to him about our common vows and the spiritual need for self -effacement in this valley of earthly tears, but he just laughed at me and called me a company fart. I told him that I would forgive him this insult, turn the other cheek, whip myself daily for the welfare of his soul, and hear his confession. Again he merely laughed and said he was sinless. I am afraid Padre Punt has gone more native than most.

I realize daily the awesome nature of my task, even if my colleagues cannot. Except in the most provincial sense, that is, the here and now of the flesh, these men do not exist, unless they be named in my history. If I choose to ignore them, then they shall not have lived. This is equivalent to God's power. Even as his Holy Name shall be synonymous with creation, so shall my name be synonymous with erasure.

This, then, is the last stage of enlightenment for the official historian of an age: the realization that one's true audience has probably not yet been born. To be caught in the seraglio of circumstance, thus, and to keep one's eye on the horizon of posterity, that is the historian's dilemma. This most awesome awareness is accompanied by a kind of ludic transcendence, a spirit of free play that ennobles my work. I become aware of my prose style, my choice of words as much as my choice of subjects, and even perhaps my duty to entertain my unborn audience, who may not give a fig about Aztec civilization.

So, then, a joke: How can you tell the bride at an Aztec wedding?—She's the one with rollers under her arms. Or: How does an Aztec woman know she's had an orgasm?—She wakes up from dreaming.

✳

My name is Ariel Lagrimas, and I am the only woman to come on this expedition of discovery to the New World. To do this, I have had to pose as a man. When Cortez agreed to take the giant Trucha as part of his crew, he also agreed to take me. I think this was his own private joke: Trucha's thunderous weight, my slight build, the one to balance the other. But I knew that I would be the butt of many jokes as a boyish, even effeminate tar, so I had to find a way to distance myself from the rest of the crew. Thus did I come as the chronic bed wetter Curcio.

At first, Cortez took pity on me and my plight, because he felt responsible for having chosen me. He began to seek me out, to tell me stories of drought in vast deserts, plying me with dryness to curb my discomfort. Never once did he make fun of me nor did he tolerate any jokes at my expense. And when he ran out of stories that were true, he began to make them up. He told me of magical lands to the south, where the forests were wet and the coastline was dry, so dry that the fountains spouted sand and the inhabitants overcame their need for water.

Gradually, Cortez looked for my company for himself, perhaps to take his mind off larger worries. For long hours at night we would sit together on the deck and look at the constellations or listen to the waves. Both of us were short and wiry, and I think he appreciated the sense of equality he felt, standing next to someone his own height.

And finally, off the coast of Cuba, he was slightly crazy with fever, and he put his arm around my waist. He told me how fair were my features, how sweet the sound of my voice, how graceful my steps amid the crew of ruffians and clods. He said my waist felt like the belt of Orion, and I felt sorry for him. He talked about transgression as though it were a trapped animal inside him, with loneliness, world-weary loneliness, as its only just excuse for bolting through his skin. He could not fathom this sudden attraction to a member of his own sex, and I couldn't put his fears to rest without risking my own life. I pretended to be sick with fever until we landed at Cozumel.

Luckily for me, Cortez was busy learning the Maya language form Geronimo de Aguilar, a priest who had been shipwrecked there seven years earlier. I always thought of Geronimo as the embodiment of Tiresias in the old myths, who, seven years here and seven years there, lived more a life of omens and dreams than one of flesh and blood.

And anon was Cortez given an Indian mistress named La Malinche, who served as our interpreter and who begat Cortez a son named Martin, the first mestizo.

I think Cortez was so grateful to be securely heterosexual again that he gave himself fully to his new family life and forgot about me. Not La Malinche. She looked at me the way Aztec high priests look at sacrifice. With one eye on the victim and the other on the gods. La Malinche was born with an inexact starobism of vision, by which she could focus on several things at once. She seemed able to look straight through my natural mustache. She seemed to stare beyond my chest armor to the pressed breasts behind. And later on, I think she stepped into my dreams once or twice.

It wasn't that she was jealous of Cortez, for Indian women seem incapable of jealousy, perhaps because of drugs and trances. It was rather that she caught me in the curiosity of her eye, so different from other Hispanic men, and maybe she knew I was a woman, maybe she knew my history with her husband, or maybe she fell in love with me a little bit, herself.

In Cozumel we saw our first human sacrifice. La Malinche told us that her gods were thirsty, and at first we thought she meant the land was dry and full of drought. But the shaman invited us to eat a woman he had sacrificed earlier that day. Cortez protested that all Europeans were vegetarians, and we were able to eat flour tortillas and corn-bean casseroles for a while. But Geronimo de Aguilar got into a drunken bragging brawl with the shaman about whose "magic" was stronger, and the shaman insisted that he could show a man his own heart, something that Geronimo had to admit was a tricky thing for the Christ to do, even in the best of his biblical exploits.

So, the stage was set, and the shaman chose a Franciscan priest named Cantinflas for his test case. He regaled Cantinflas for three days and nights, feeding him extra helpings of beans and rice as well as massaging his whole body with eucalyptus oils every night. Cantinflas traded in his brown sackcloth for royal robes and a red headdress of cockatoo and macaw. The unsuspecting Cantinflas was so enamored of his new status that he forgot to say his vespers and matins.

On the third night the shaman coaxed Cantinflas into a drunken stupor with a mixture of hot tequila toddy, peyote and bitter chocolate laced with novocaine. La Malinche knew the ingredients, for she was something of a practiced shaman, herself, and she patiently described every detail of this ritual, without ever once trying to stop it.

Finally, around midnight we all climbed to the upper parapet of the local pyramids, and there the shaman convinced Cantinflas that he should disrobe and learn how to fly like a bird. The dizzy Franciscan was so prone to suggestion that he stripped immediately and began to flap his arms at his sides.

"Can you feel anything?" the shaman asked in a country dialect Nahuatl, the language of the Aztecs.

La Malinche translated.

"Pues nada," Cantinflas said, and La Malinche translated.

"But I just stuck a needle in your back," the shaman said.

And so he did. But Cantinflas laughed and said he felt nothing but the wind at his back and the stars for his halo. So the shaman proposed to show Cantinflas his heart and the flapping Franciscan agreed.

So the shaman cut a hole in Cantinflas' chest and plucked out the poor man's heart, putting the bloody palpitating organ up to Cantinflas' eyes.

"Un milagro," Cantinflas shouted, numb, dumbstruck, quite heartless, and then quickly dead.

Most of the tars thought it was a New World joke, and they kept waiting for the shaman to put the heart back, but the shaman said the heart belonged to him now, and he would stir-fry the body for breakfast, eating the foreigner's God as well as the man.

The whole experience was so exhilarating that nobody tried to stop him. Cortez was afraid of offending La Malinche, who seemed to approve of the custom.

Gradually, I learned that young boys and able-bodied men were rarely slaughtered for sacrifice, since they were the warrior class of the Aztecs. That left lame men, barren women and young girls as the victims, and the ritual was always the same: fatten them up, fleece them of feelings with ointment and drugs, then cut their hearts out for all the thirsty gods to savor.

It fell on me, then, to form the first underground railroad in the New World. I helped the Aztec mothers to hide their female babies in the bulrushes. I taught the young girls to hide their sex, to dress and act like boys. I helped barren women stuff their robes with chicken feathers and goose down, feigning pregnancy. And I coached lame men to hide their disabilities: A shorter leg could wear a longer shoe, a cleft palate could be taught to skip speech and sing instead, and the deaf could be shown how to put a large conch to their ears and pretend to be listening. And when each ruse became precarious, I found ways to sneak them down South, beyond the Aztec Empire and the Toltec taste for human blood.

Some of the shamans countered by inventing wars in which new men would be maimed or by stealing babies from their mothers or poking needles into old women's supposedly pregnant stomachs while they slept. The sacrifices and ensuing cannibalism continued thus, but not without much guile on both sides.

Yet, even in the palace of the great Montezuma, some of the women began to organize and wonder aloud why being female meant that they would became food one day. And some of them resorted to the most imaginative methods to forestall their fate. One cut the heel off the left shoe of her husband, to make him appear lame the next day. Another put thistle in her brother's food, to make him appear to speak with a lisp. Yet another shone mirrors on her father-in-law's eyes during his siesta, so that he seemed to wake up blind. Thus did the women make their men lame, giving them a taste of their own medicine.

Those women who walked in dreams, remaining semi-conscious on their brew of steeped bitter chocolate and hot chilis, were beyond our help. We knew them by their brown mouths and missing teeth. They were eventually slaughtered.

One night La Malinche stepped into one of my dreams and spoke to me.

"Ariel Lagrimas," she wailed.

"You know me, then?"

"You are woman," she said in flawless Castellano.

"Yet you are neither *pan* like the Aztecs nor macho like the Hispanics. You are *machopan*. You are mix of *pasodoble* and *pesadumbre,* no? You are *sol y sombra. Nuit et brouillard. Sturm und drang. Lagrimas et risas.* "

She went on for a long while with this litany of opposites in tongues, and I neither stopped her nor encouraged her, confirmed or denied, concealed or revealed. When she called me a myth, I interrupted.

"Pinche Malinche," I said, trying to cast some spell of my own, "are we not all women in the womb before some of us are doomed to be men?"

My argument must have distracted her, because she stopped pointing at me like some harpy scarecrow and began to smile from guileless teeth.

"How did you grow that natural mustache she asked, full of approval now.

I told her about eating oysters, bull brains, mandrake and other macho things.

We talked about women's clothes and wampum beads for a while, agreed to exchange wardrobes, and finally came to the conclusion that Hispanics should never have come to the New World.

"*Mestizo* mess," she said, spitting out some peanut shells between words. She went on to say that neither of our races was pure any longer, and no good could come from the potpourri. She went so far as to curse the result, including her own son Martin, who was spotty-brown and couldn't decide whether he should be a conquistador or a concierge when he grew up, calling all *mestizos* "Hispaztecs." She cleaned several glots of congealed peanuts from between her teeth with her fingers, and then she spat again, metaphorically as well as physically.

"*Leche-dereche y mierda-izquierda*," she said.

I was amazed at her command of idiomatic Castellano.

"I suppose you'll be marrying an Aztec sooner or later," she said, already too resigned to the idea for my tastes.

"No," I said. "I never will marry."

"Madre-Nevada," she shouted with obvious joy, repeating her husband's favorite phrase.

"I suppose you're going to turn me in," I said, already resigning myself to that climb up the pyramids.

"Never happen," she laughed. "We women have to stick together."

✳

Salvete Rex et Regina et discipuli mundi. I am Escondido, the navigator for Cortez in the New World. Once we landed, of course, I had little need of my navigational skills, so I began teaching Latin to the Aztecs. I teach Latin, but I am not a priest. I want to make that perfectly clear. I am one of the few lay Latin teachers in the Western World, I have my certification for primary and secondary education, and I come by it honestly.

The Aztecs have taken to my teaching with a modicum of enthusiasm that is rare for them. Latin is a dead language, and the Aztecs like things that pertain to the dead. And, in terms of transformational grammar, I have found that there are more similarities between Latin and Nahuatl than between Spanish and Nahuatl or Spanish and Latin.

My students are mostly young boys of the warrior class. They come in face paint, scantily clad and ready for bear. They enjoy transpositions from the classic texts. For example, the use of the passive periphrastic, as in "*Cozumel delenda est*" or the use of fractional historical narratives, as in "*Chichen Itza divisa est en tres partes.*"

The Aztecs also prefer vocabulary lists to sentence-building, as they often speak in sentence fragments, especially when using dead languages like Latin. This is a sample list:

puerile
fulcrum
pulchritude
bellicose
conundrum
pugilist

latifundios
mordida
mater
nevadum

The Aztecs are also crackerjack spellers. Montezuma, himself, won the first spelling bee, correctly spelling "monosodium glutamate" and "infectious hepatitis."

Left to their own devices, the Aztecs would prefer to learn Latin in the laid-back fashion of trance states and dreams, waiting for Caesar or Ovid to appear to them. They need prodding, and they respond well to pressure. They like pop quizzes.

Their own literature is largely *mestizo,* Dada and scattered. They put a lot of stock in captivity narratives and stream-of-consciousness by the possessed. The cost of fame is high, though. One of their novelists, Rulfo, became a drunken dreamspeaker after a successful first novel. Another, Fuentes, expatriated himself. Still another, Pax Octavian, took a Latin name and then joined the Foreign Legion. Apparently, it is a severe shock to the Aztec psyche to communicate in the fine arts. And so most of their best-known artists have led fairly tragic lives.

Much of the problem stems from the multiplicity of diminutives used in seemingly incongruous ways. For example, in Spain we say "*hijo de la puta,*" which means "son of a whore." But in Tenochtitlán and Tlatelolco they say "*hijo de la chingada,*" which means "son of a raped woman." The sense of rape permeates the entire culture.

More telling perhaps is the fact that nobody knows who's who in the family, precisely because of all the linguistic shifters. A woman will call her son "*papito*" ("little father") and her husband "*mi hijo*" ("my son"). We may have forced the Aztecs to learn our Spanish language, but they have chosen to learn it in their own idiosyncratic way.

Painting is equally ambiguous. Pre-Hispanic paintings

illustrated conversations by means of floating balloons, hovering in space and detached from the speakers, as though words had a life of their own, independent of their utterance. The paintings are an incredible array of the most gaudy-bulbous primary colors and pastels. Of the four walls in an Aztec bedroom, it is not uncommon to find one in pink, another purple, another green and the last burnt henna or a rather melancholy cadmium blue. They excel in temple building and pudgy-wonderful pyramids, their architecture is most always more aesthetic than functional, and their murals depict famous battles, various shapes the deities have taken, and samples of human sacrifice, and, so, their walls are a kind of walking *Iliad* and *Odyssey* of the Aztec nation. In one of the most famous murals, Cortez is portrayed as a syphilitic hunchback. Otherwise, the only commemoration of the conquest is a bust of Cortez in the Casino de la Selva in Cuernevaca.

That bust owes its existence in a peculiar way to that mawkish missed-historian Gaspar de Carvelho, who decided one day that we should rename Cuernevaca Torremolinos.

If we began baptizing all their city-states with Iberian names, he argued, then one day the Aztecs would have for a president someone named Ferdinand or Isabella or de la Madrid. Cortez liked the idea, and we exped-itioned to Cuernevaca with the sole purpose of renaming it Torremolinos, but the Cuernevacans had gotten wind of the scheme and had hurried up a bust of the conquistador. Cortez was so pleased with the likeness that he let Cuernevaca keep its name.

On that same expedition we went to Cancún, and there on the white warm beaches Cortez ordained that the first beauty contest be held in the New World. Young girls twixt twelve and twenty were ordered to wear Spanish bathing suits and parade at low tide. That chronic bed-wetter Curcio was chosen to judge the contest. He chose the ugliest one of the lot, a surly wench named Alfredisia, who had the hips of a baobab tree, no teeth and earrings that were bigger than arm bracelets. When asked about his selection, Curcio praised the dryness of the Aztec skin and said Alfredisia evidenced more dandruff than the others. Cortez upheld Curcio's decision, and Alfredisia was crowned Queen of Cancún for a day.

The Aztecs cared a great deal about beauty, but they cared not at all for a beauty contest on the beaches of Cancún and judged by a chronic bedwetter like Curcio. They referred to the whole ordeal as *mitotero,* the act of creating myths to exaggerate one's own importance, and they summarily sacrificed Alfredisia and ate her.

In a similar vein they seemed willing to intermarry with Hispanics, but only for the purpose of procreation. They resisted rigidly assigned roles like *marido* ("husband") and *eposa* ("wife") and simply referred to the couple as *mariposa,* which, of course, means "butterfly," the concept of which was not inconsistent with those detached balloons in their murals.

Now a swelling melancholy has infected both the Spanish and the Aztecs, as though the mixing of the two bloods had inevitably to become this sad puree. My students are grade-conscious, but only spasmodically so. They want to be *licenciados* in Latin, and they do not understand their overall deficiencies in the liberal arts program. They love those texts which deal with the reign of Nero and the lions devouring the Christians, but they are phlegmatic about the pastoral poems and epigrams.

Then, too, there is occasional interference from the outside. From time to time one of my students is maimed in combat and is then chosen by the shaman for sacrifice, and I have to record permanent incompletes for these students. The toadstool Gaspar thinks that Latin can only be taught by the clergy, and he questions my authority as a lay Latin teacher. Quemada has told my students that he is the reincarnation of Nero, and he reserves the right to set them on fire any time he chooses. The charismatic Padre Punt wants Latin abolished from the curriculum, unless it can be incorporated into a more interdisciplinary course in speaking-in-tongues. And Jaime Posado and the commoners among the crew have filed official protests with Cortez that teaching Latin to the Aztecs constitutes racial discrimination, intellectual pandering and elitism of the worst sort.

For my part, I resist and will continue to resist any interference of this kind. Teaching Latin is a sacred occupation, and, if any of these barbarians think I'm going to navigate them back to Spain some day, they have another think coming.

※

I am Anónimo, the poet laureate of the court of Spain, and I was sent on this expedition to capture the thrill of victory and the agony of defeat, but I have nothing to say at this point.

※

I am Huizinga. I am Dutch and I set sail on a Dutch Reform pirate ship for Hudson Bay, but we had a bad navigator, and ended up shipwrecked off the coast of Cuba, whereupon every member of our crew was either eaten by cannibals or executed by the Spanish Viceroy and his troops. I alone survived the decimation, hiding out in the sugar cane fields, until the crew of Cortez found me half-naked and so sugarswilled that they mistook me for an Indian, Inca or Aztec or Oxenard. I said words like *"zum"* and *"zulu"* and let them think what they liked, and the incredibly gullible Cortez saw in me an omen of good fortune and decided to proceed to Mexico instead of returning to Spain, as his King had ordered.

The Spaniards do not know me as Huizinga. They know me as Huxaca, and I am content to leave them in their wrong assumption.

I came to the New World to escape religious intolerance

and to practice radical thinking whenever I chose. Instead, I have involuntarily surrounded myself with charlatans and zealots, heretics and headhunters on both sides. It is difficult to choose between the shamans and the Jesuits as to which one is more bloodthirsty or superstitious. The shamans practice human sacrifice and view everyone as a prospective meal. The Jesuits buy and sell indulgences in exchange for local pottery, and they practice exotic tortures when they are hard-pressed or bored. Padre Punt has asked me to enroll in his growing charismatic congregation and to participate in gospel chanting and fundamentalist square dancing. The blowhard historian Gaspar has asked me to gather data and local jokes for him. And the firebrand Quemada wants me to aid and abet him in a countrywide campaign to burn all the livestock and crops. They are all crazy.

The Spanish think I should live with the Aztecs, because they think I am an Indian, while the Aztecs think I should live with the Spanish, because they know better. I am a man without a country, shunned by both sides.

I am further compromised as well. I am secretly in love with a sinewy boy named Curcio, who, it turns out, is a chronic bedwetter, a malady which I do not hold against him in any way. But I am afraid of declaring my true feelings, for fear that Curcio, who has access to the ear of Cortez, might have me found out and flogged by the Spanish or, worse yet, sacrificed by the shamans.

Out of my nostalgia for the Zuider Zee, I built a windmill on my given plot of land and irrigated the soil all around the little manmade canals. Cortez was impressed with this sudden display of Europeanization from a wayward Indian, and he called it a miracle. I wanted to vomit on this overly Catholic interpretation of my behavior, but I dared not.

In desperation I went to Montezuma and told him who I was. He was neither impressed nor disillusioned. He had thought Cortez to be the reincarnation of Quetzalcoatl, the plumed serpent and the White God of Gods, and he had already paid dearly for that mistake. As long as I wasn't a returning Aztec God, he said, he didn't care who I was or what became of me.

I became melancholy. Cerebella, the official jester on this expedition, tried to cheer me up with pranks and pratfalls, but, of course, it was his job to do so, and I was not ultimately cheered.

"What kind of jokes do you like?" he asked. "Aztec or Spanish? I can do both."

"Neither," I said. "I like religious jokes."

"Okay," he said. "Did you hear the one about the Pope who told this rich land baron that he was infallible, and the rich baron says, 'Oh yeah? So who owns this land? Me or God?' And the Pope says, "I don't know. I'll have to check with my realtor.'"

"That's not funny. Do you know any jokes about the English?"

"Let's see. What's the difference between mad dogs and Englishmen?"

"I don't know."

"That's just it. They don't either."

"That's not funny. Why don't you go ask the shaman what's for supper?"

Cerebella emoted a mock pout, did a backwards somersault, and went off chasing an armadillo.

My pain remains. I want to start a revolution, but, between the prolific decadence of the Spaniards and the fierce unpredictability of the Aztecs, I don't know how. I simply don't know how. I feel somewhat *de trop,* as the French are fond of saying.

Noticing my melancholy, Cortez ordered a sweeping for me. Mix of Catholic exorcism and Aztec janitorial voodoo, a sweeping is a temple ritual, in which a shaman surrounds the person to be swept with frankincense and myrrh and, using broomwheat as his instrument, he sweeps away all sins and evil demons. The shaman Zigeroa performed this sweeping upon my person, eradicating all physical traces of ill will.

And yet my pain remains, resistant to Mexican ritual. I am determined to go North the first chance I can. New Rochelle cannot be more than five- or ten-thousand miles away.

✱

This is Anónimo again, and I still have nothing to say.

I think speaking in tongues is the only true international language, the language of love, God's real intentions behind Babel. Jump, kick heels, dance and sing, this is my mission. Shout, shout and shout again in Jesus' holy name. Call him Quetzalcoatl if you've a mind to. What's in a name?

I am Padre Punt.

✱

I want to speak.

I want to speak about the power of our pagan gods.

I call upon the power of our pagan gods, because I, myself, am supposed to be a god. But the ancient gods have answered me with silence, and I have betrayed my people. I have sent my once proud people into bondage.

My name is Moctezuma, not Montezuma, as I am called by the Hispanics. In 1502 I became the High Priest of Huitzilopochtli, and in that time our gods all spoke to me. Huitzilopochtli, the God of War, he spoke to me. Tlaloc, the God of Water, he spoke to me. And everywhere on the islands of Tenochtitlán and Tlatelolco, our palaces were filled with gold, our people ate fish daily, the monkeys roamed freely in the banana trees, and the sea was still filled with liquid emeralds. Now the sea is murky-red with Aztec blood.

I considered Quetzalcoatl to be the brother of my soul. My dreamspeaker. The White God. The Plumed Snake, he who gave invention to agriculture, astronomy, medicine, and even the royalty with which I wrapped myself. Quetzalcoatl was the first to banish the blood sacrifice in our tribe, for which he was tricked into breaking his vow of chastity, then shamed, then forced into exile.

I have waited all my life for his return. I thought that the nighthawk brought me my brother in the form of this monster Cortez. I opened the gates to our cities to this mere mortal, offered him all the hospitality at my disposal. He ate and drank with me as my honored guest, and then he arrested me in my own palace. Instead of calling for my guards to behead him and his men, I waited for a sign from my gods. Was this not, then, the Quetzalcoatl I had awaited all the years of my life? Was this merely, then, the most vulgar of foreign devils, come to tempt me in my time of longing? Or perhaps was this a test by Quetzatcoatl, to see if I could humble myself before him and all my subjects, after which he would cease acting like a vapid little pirate and reveal himself in all his splendor and plumage? I could not believe that I had been deceived, and so I allowed myself to be arrested by the Spaniard.

The Aztec people have not believed in their gods since that day. Seeing me shackled and expelled from my own palace was a shock too great for my people to bear. The fierce warrior is the first to fall when he trusts in the past.

In that manner did Quetzalcoatl appear to me in dreams as the coiled snake. He said that we had indeed become brothers of the blood and soul, for I, too, now knew the taste of shame and the proud betrayal of all ancestral gods. They would still exact their blood sacrifice, he said, but they would never again speak to the High Priest who ruled the Aztecs. I protested that they had been silent even before the coming of the conquistador, and he replied that their silence was the real test, not the coming of the Spaniard.

Was it not possible, then, to reclaim the godhead for myself, I asked. No, he hissed, it was no longer possible. It would never again be possible, and I would have to understand that even gods as great as he suffered many deaths, the last of which was the loss of all human memory of them. Was he not already banished to visiting me in dreams? Would he not have come in person if he could have found the power to do so?

And was it so inevitable, this waning of power? Yes, he answered, but, for every decrease in power, there was an increase in wisdom. Only the most powerful gods would stoop to meddle in human combat. The wisest gods were the most disembodied. These gods took the form of the space between the stars.

I asked his forgiveness for surrendering to the Spaniard, but he did not understand this request. A god, to be a god, never asked forgiveness. Was this not my proof that I had become mortal by surrendering to a mortal? And was this not punishment enough, retribution beyond the need for forgiveness, to know that I would die a mortal death, a slave's death?

I asked if one day the grandchildren of my grandchildren, having married one Spaniard after another, might not return to Spain as conquerors and form a new and stronger Aztec Empire across the ocean? Perhaps, he said, but the old gods would not go with them. Instead, the Christian god would have his churches built side-by-side with Aztec temples, its missions side-by-side with our pyramids, its priests side-by-side with our shamans, until the grandchildren of our grandchildren would mistake the one for the other.

"You are mortal now," he said, "and you will be remembered and then forgotten as a mortal, but, while your heart still lives, I am the last of the old gods to live through you. I shall die when you die. This is your power."

When I made no answer, he fell silent and disappeared from my dreams forever.

✻

"The Spanish are troubled with a disease of the heart, for which gold is a specific remedy."

I said this. The sentence has been ascribed to me, and I do not deny saying it. Over time, it has lost the irony with which I said it.

I was thirty-five when we set sail from Cuba in 1519 with five hundred men and sixteen horses aboard ten galleons. I was surprised when we found the shipwrecked priest Geronimo de Aguilar in Cozumel. We found this country wild with strife and local rebellions against the Aztecs. We gained new allies everywhere we went, due in no small part to the influence of my wife and interpreter La Malinche.

It is true that I arrested Montezuma in his own palace and that twelve million Aztecs stood by and let five-hundred Spaniards enslave them.

But perhaps it is easier to be the conquered than to be the conqueror. I gained no thanks from Spain for having conquered the entire Aztec Empire without a single shot fired. I was perceived as a rebel. Even as I arrested Montezuma in his palace, new galleons were leaving ports in Spain with orders to replace me.

And I am a conqueror, not a ruler. I gave whole kingdoms to my men and they abused them with bloodshed and corruption. I had to leave Tenochtitlán to quell a rebellion by Jaime Posado. I had handpicked Posado, myself, only to be forced to execute him for this rebellion. Many Spaniards died on both sides.

When I came back to Tenochtitlán, the Aztecs had erupted. They had killed my giant, Gabriel Trucha, and were eating his various parts without any regard for my feelings in the matter. I convinced Montezuma to speak to them from the palace balcony and to plead for peace, but his subjects stoned him and he died.

His successor, Cuauhtomoc, was more surly and rebellious than ever Montezuma had been. Each time I left the islands to fight this or that border war, I would come back to armed Aztecs and more insurrection. They hung the head of Padre Punt on the end of a spear and teased the bulls with it.

They cut off the fingers of Gaspar de Carvelho, my appointed historian. The only Spaniards they seemed to tolerate were the clown Cerebella and the fair bed-wetter Curcio.

When Montezuma died, there was chaos all around. I could barely control my own men, who during the night we now call "la noche triste" tried to leave the causeways and drowned, overloaded with gold. Cuauht6moc fled as well, taking hope in the death of so many Spaniards. He said it was the revenge of Tlaloc, their God of Water, who swallowed up so many Spaniards and their greed.

We pursued Cuauhtémoc, with the loyal Quemada in charge of my troops, and on August 13, 1521, the pyramids of Tlatelolco, defended by Cuauhtémoc and his warriors, fell to our army.

And still Cuauhtémoc was not contrite.   Quemada convinced me that we should burn his feet off, and we did that, in hope of extracting the secret of the vast treasure troves of Aztec gold, but he would not speak.

We never did find the gold.

Later, Quemada accused Cuauhtémoc of treason, and we had him hung in the public square, to the embarrassment of all his people.

When we left Veracruz, we were met by the replacement armies from Spain, and I was ousted as governor and forced into semi-retirement at my hacienda on the banks of Lake Texcoco.

These are the historical facts of our expedition.

It is true that we slaughtered many Aztecs during the Conquest, and it is also true that eventually they killed many of us. And who dares to understand such carnage, who has not been there? There were reasons, and they seemed like good reasons at the time, but now I am old, living in exile in the land I conquered, with blood on my conscience.

I regret most the death of Montezuma, who was in many ways the most enlightened ruler I have ever met. He had many qualities to which I aspired and sadly never attained. He was a god when I met him and a slave when I left him. And yet, through all the incidents of humiliation, he never lost his dignity. I wanted somehow to understand him and be understood by him, but we were on opposite sides of the some coin.

If circumstances had been different and I had been born an Aztec, I would have sailed for him and conquered Spain. Instead, I am left with this memory of the man: that he ate fish daily instead of human flesh.

I want to speak of loneliness. The loneliness of conquerors. The glory that is as fleeting as the seasons. There are no words to describe the solitude of warriors. What I have seen and felt and done is cloaked in silence now.

I have built my house on the banks of Lake Texcoco. The architects were Spanish. The laborers were Aztec. And so my house is in the *mestizo* style that my successors pretentiously call "Mexican colonial": both ornately baroque and wildly Aztec. And deeply melancholy.

✴

I am Cerebella, the jester, and I am the only one who got rich in the New World.

I knew the true identities of everyone, but I said nothing. Histories will call him Hernando Cortez, but I knew him to be Hernán Cortés. I knew Ariel Lagrimas for the wondrous woman she was behind the damp boy's clothes. I knew Huizinga was a bowlegged Dutchman and not a lost Incan, and I goaded that man to distraction with bad jokes and pratfalls. I knew the true posture of every single man, woman and child, Spanish or Aztec, and I made them laugh on both sides.

Cortés was not a malicious man. He was skilled in combat, daring, superstitious, and sensitive about his age and height. But he was not an enlightened man. His vision never extended beyond the day he was living and the crisis at the end of his nose.

Things went badly for Cortés in the end. He went back to Spain finally, and he died there. His heart was broken, his memory was slandered. The Aztecs told lies and legends about him, which the court of Spain chose to believe. In the end he was totally shunned.

The bloody deeds ascribed to him were mostly done by Quemada. And the few kind deeds attributed to him were the work of Ariel Lagrimas. Quemada and Ariel Lagrimas, they were Cortés' angels of darkness and light. I never could make Quemada laugh and I never could make Ariel Lagrimas blush from her disguise. This is how I will remember them both.

In 1547 the bones of Cortés were returned to Mexico and put to rest there at the Hospital de Jésus, which he founded. Absolutely nobody will remember him for the founding of any hospitals.

We never found the Aztecs' gold. We stole just enough of it to know there was more, so much more, we couldn't find. Cortés wanted the gold, not for himself, but rather as the price of forgiveness for having disobeyed his King and Queen. The gold would have been the proof of his worth. He would have made them the richest monarchs in the Western world. But the vast stockpiles of gold eluded us. They were as much the stuff of Maya and illusion as any myths told about us.

I think I know where all that gold lay. I think it was right under our noses all the time. Indeed, I suspect that the Aztecs sun-baked it into the stones they used for the pyramids, those very pyramids we tried so hard to avoid, because they were synonymous with human blood sacrifice for us.

I have no interest in the gold now. I am rich beyond my wildest dreams, as rich as any man in Europe. It wasn't any gold I took back with me, but the chocolate we discovered in Mexico. The Aztecs took it as a drug, mixed with hot peppers and peyote, a concoction too bitter for any European palate.

In all the years of the Conquest, this concoction was perhaps the only Aztec thing we didn't usurp.

I got the idea for sweetening the chocolate from Huizinga, who chewed on sugar cane the way squirrels nibble acorns. I brought the bitter chocolate back to Spain with me, refined it with milk, softened its texture, sun-dried it and sweetened it with sugar. In solid form or liquid form there is not man or woman of wealth in every country on the continent who has not tasted my sweet chocolate and developed an addiction for it, not unlike the greed with which we went after the Aztecs' gold.

The history books will not record my discovery. I don't care. Cortés will be remembered, however falsely, and I will be forgotten. I don't care. I will have entered the houses and mouths of every living person on this planet, a feat which not even the wisest and most ancient of the Aztec gods could pretend to.

The laughter is all mine now.